LVE

IN THE TIME OF
GLOBAL
WARMING

FRANCESCA
LIA BLOCK

LOVE
IN THE TIME OF
GLOBAL
WARMING

SQUARE
FISH

HENRY HOLT AND COMPANY
NEW YORK

An Imprint of Macmillan
175 Fifth Avenue
New York, NY 10010
fiercereads.com

Square Fish books may be purchased for business or promotional use. For
information on bulk purchases, please contact the Macmillan Corporate
and Premium Sales Department at (800) 221-7945 x5442 or by
e-mail at specialmarkets@macmillan.com.

Library of Congress Cataloging-in-Publication Data
Block, Francesca Lia.
Love in the time of global warming / Francesca Lia Block.
pages   cm
"Christy Ottaviano Books."
Summary: After a devastating earthquake destroys the West Coast, causing
seventeen-year-old Penelope to lose her home, her parents, and her
ten-year-old brother, she navigates a dark world, holding hope and
love in her hands and refusing to be defeated.
ISBN 978-1-250-04442-6 (paperback) / ISBN 978-0-8050-9902-7 (e-book)
[1. Survival—Fiction.   2. Families—Fiction.   3. Love—Fiction.   4. Voyages
and travels—Fiction.   5. Earthquakes—Fiction.   6. Los Angeles
(Calif.)—Fiction.   7. Science fiction.]   I. Title.
PZ7.B61945Lo 2013   [Fic]—dc23   2012047808

Originally published in the United States by Christy Ottaviano Books /
Henry Holt and Company
First Square Fish Edition: 2014
Book designed by April Ward
Square Fish logo designed by Filomena Tuosto

9   10

4 AR: 5.0 / LEXILE: 850L

For Jasmine, Sam, Jeni, and Ezekiel

Oh my child, ill-fated beyond all other mortals,
this is not Persephone, daughter of Zeus, beguiling you,
but it is only what happens when they die, to all mortals.
The sinews no longer hold the flesh and the bones together,
And once the spirit has left the white bones, all the rest
Of the body is made subject to the fire's strong fury,
But the soul flitters out like a dream and flies away.

From Homer's *The Odyssey*

THE BUILDING HAS GOLD COLUMNS and a massive doorway, a mural depicting Giants, with bodies sticking out of their mouths like limp cigarettes. Someone besides me has studied their Goya. Bank of the Apocalypse reads a handwritten sign. It balances atop a pile of ruin-rubble and clean-sucked human bones. I can make out doors and windows, crumbled fireplaces, tiles, metal pipes, shingles, signs that read Foreclosure. The homes of so many skeletons. People who used to fight over the last blueberry muffin at the breakfast table, get down on their knees to scrub bathroom floors, and kiss one another good night, thinking they were at least relatively safe. Now they are just dust in the debris.

I climb through the rubble toward the door. It takes a long time, time enough for a Giant to see me from the blood-red stained-glass eye window and reach out to crush me in his hand the size of a tractor.

My mother never foresaw this danger. She was scared we would get sick from drinking tap water, eating genetically modified fruits and vegetables, even breathing the air. We had to put on sunscreen every day because of that hole in the ozone that kept her up at night. She gave us vitamins and bought us only chemical-free shampoo, even though it never made my hair as soft and clean as Moira's. I used to hate how afraid my mom was and how afraid she had made me. Now I understand but I can no longer be like her. I have to fight.

The ceilings are so high I can't see the top of them, and the only light is from the red glass eye. All around me are vaults that look like crypts. The whole place is a mausoleum.

"Here she is," a voice says.

Not a Giant but Kronen emerges from the shadows, wearing a carefully constructed suit made of patches of dried, bumpy material. I force myself to stand my ground. The sword in my hand looks like a needle, even to me, though Kronen is only a few inches taller than I am.

"You've come back?" he says, smiling. It further distorts the uneven planes of his face. "I knew you would come back."

"I want my friends," I say. "You have my eye. You took my mother. I want to know what happened to her, and to my friends. And my brother."

"Friends are important. Brothers are important. Sons, sons are important."

"I know," I say. "I'm sorry for what I did. But you had your revenge. An eye for an eye."

"What will you give me if I don't help you find them? A stick in the eye?" he muses.

I won't let my hand go to the empty socket hiding under the patch. I won't think of how that eye is gone, how it is as if every work of art, every beloved's face it ever reflected, has vanished with it. If I saw madness in Kronen before, now it has exploded like a boil. That nasty suit—it looks like it's made of dried skin.

"If you don't tell me, if you don't return them to me safely, I will kill you," I say.

Kronen pets the strip of hair on his chin in a way that feels too intimate, almost sexual. His eyes roll up in contemplation. "I don't know where your friends are," he says cheerily. "Your dear mother died of natural causes, poor thing. Your brother got away from me." Then his voice changes, deepens, his eyes stab at my face. "And you could not kill me if you tried. Have you forgotten who I am? What I have made? What I have destroyed?"

His laughter turns into shaking and the shaking comes from the steps of the Giant entering the room.

Now my sword really is a needle. And the color of fear dripping through my veins? Like our old friend, Homer, said, fear is green.

1

THE EARTH SHAKER

THE ROOM WAS SHAKING and I thought I knew what it was because I had been born and raised in a city built on fault lines. Everyone was always dreading something like this. But we never imagined it would be of such force and magnitude.

I called to Venice, the most beautiful, smartest, sweetest (and he would want me to add most athletic) boy in the world, "I'm coming! Are you okay?"

I imagined his body lying under boards and glass, pinned down, but when I got to him he was just huddled in the bed in the room papered with maps of the world, wearing the baseball cap he insisted on sleeping in (in spite of the stiff bill), trembling so hard I could barely gather him up in my arms. My dad came in and took him from me—my brother's legs in too short pajama pants dangling down, his face buried in my dad's neck as Venice cried for his fallen cap—and I got our dog, Argos, and we all ran downstairs. My mom was there, crying, and she grabbed me and I could feel her heart like a frantic butterfly through her white cotton nightgown. We ran out into the yard. The sky looked black and dead without the streetlight or the blue Christmas lights that decked our house. I could hear the ocean crashing, too close, too close. The world sliding away from us.

The tall acacia tree in the yard creaked and moaned, and then my ears rang with the silence before danger. My dad pulled us back as we watched the tree crash to the ground in a shudder of leaves and branches. My tree, the one I had strung with gold fairy lights, the one that shaded parties made for teddy bears and dolls, the tree in whose pink-blossomed branches Dad had built a wooden platform house with a rope ladder. That was where I went to read art history books and mythology, and to escape the world that now I only wanted to save.

I was holding Argos and he wriggled free and jumped down and ran away from me, toward our big pink house overgrown with morning glory vines and electric wires strung with glass bulbs. I screamed for him and my mom tried to hold me back but I was already running. I was inside.

The floor was paved with broken glass from the Christmas ornaments and family photos that had fallen. (A tall man with wild, sandy-colored hair and tanned, capable hands, a curvy, olive-skinned woman with gray eyes, an unremarkable teenage girl, an astonishingly handsome boy and a dog that was a mix of so many odd breeds it made you laugh to look at him.) My feet were bare. I reached for a pair of my mother's suede and shearling boots by the door, yanked them on, and stepped over the glass, calling for my dog. He was yelping and growling at an invisible phantom; his paws were bleeding. I picked him up and blood streaked down my legs.

I turned to open the door but a wall of water surged toward me behind the glass pane and I put up my hands as if to hold it back, as if to part the wave.

And then I fell.

That's all I remember of the last day of the life I once knew.

2

THE PINK HAND
OF DAWN

WHEN I WAKE EACH MORNING—Venice's baseball cap beside me and a photo of my family under my pillow—and feel the pink hand of dawn stroking my face, sometimes I forget that my mother and father and Venice and Argos are gone, that my best friends Moira and Noey are gone. I forget that I am alone here in this house, with the sea roiling squid-ink purple-black, dark like a witch's brew, just outside my window, where once there existed the rest of my city, now lost as far as I can see. Even dawn is a rare thing, for usually the sky is too thick with smoke for me to see the sun rise.

When I did go outside, after the water levels went

down, the smoke-black air, and the piles of rubble that had once been buildings, were the first things I noticed. Then I saw the giant frightful clown in the blue ballerina tutu; he used to preside over the city of Venice and now bobbed in the water among a banquet of Styrofoam cups and plastic containers. He was missing one white-gloved hand but still had his red top hat and bulbous nose, his black beard. The clown had made me drop my ice cream and run screaming to my mother when I was a child; now he looked even more monstrous. I saw crushed cars stacked on top of one another and the street in front of my house split in two, exposing the innards of the earth. Nothing grew and not a soul roamed. The trees had fallen and the ground was barren of any life, the world as far as I could see, deserted.

The debris of splintered buildings floated in swamps that were once the neighborhood where my friends lived. Moira's family's green and white Craftsman bungalow vanished; Noey's mother's 1960s apartment washed away. Had my friends run screaming, barefoot in their pajamas, from their houses into the street? If I listened, could I have heard their voices beneath the crash of the surf? Had they been killed in their sleep? Were they conscious when it happened, were they in pain?

I think of Moira's ginger hair. Was it loose or braided? She sometimes braided it when she slept. I can see Noey's watchful artist's eyes, so round and brown in her round, dimpled face. Was she wearing one of her vintage punk T-shirts and men's striped silk pajama pants? I can pretend my friends are somewhere out there alive but sometimes hope only makes everything worse.

It's been fifty-three days since the Earth Shaker— I've ticked them off with red marks on the wall by my bed as if this small ritual will restore some meaning to my life. It's early February but that doesn't signify much anymore. No bills to pay, no homework due, no holidays. If things were different I might have been collaging Valentines for Moira and Noey and buying dense chocolate hearts wrapped in crinkle-shiny red paper for Venice.

I've cleaned the house as best I can, sweeping up the glass, nailing down loose boards. I tried to avoid bathing for as long as possible but finally, when the crust on my skin hurt, I gave in and now I use a minimal amount of the precious bottled spring water with which my anxious (overly, I once thought) father stocked the basement for a sponge bath every week and a half. I eat as little as possible from my father's stockpile of canned foods to make them last. No one has come for me this whole time, which makes me think that this disaster reaches farther than I can see. But who knows what would happen if a stranger came. Perhaps I'm better off this way.

In the morning I try to make this half-dream state last, imagining Argos licking my face the way he was not allowed to do, because it might make me break out, but I let him anyway. Then I flip him over so he is on top of me, his body stretched out, belly exposed, big paws flopping, his tongue still trying to reach me from the side of his mouth, even in this position. Above us, the da Vinci, Vermeer, Picasso, Van Gogh, Matisse, and O'Keeffe prints (torn from broken-backed art books found at garage sales) papered the low attic ceiling like a heaven of great masterworks. (They are still here, though damp and peeling away from the wood.)

I imagine my mother calling me from downstairs that breakfast is ready and I am going to be late for school, calling for Venice to stop playing video games and come down and eat. I cannot smell, but I try to imagine, the scent of homemade bread and eggs cooked in butter, the mix of sweet jasmine and tangy eucalyptus leaves baking in the sun. The sharp smell of turpentine in which my mother's paintbrushes soak, the sight of her latest canvas on the easel—a two-story pink house in a storm on the edge of a cliff with a sweet-faced boy peering out the window. The sound of the sprinklers zizzing on outside, the throaty coo of doves in the trees.

I tell myself that when I get up and go downstairs my mother will say, "Brush your hair, Penelope. You can't go to school like that." This time I will not make a comment, but kiss her cheek and go back up and do it, thinking of how Moira spends hours each morning straightening her hair sleek and how Noey's black pixie cut is too short to need a fuss. I will eat the oatmeal without complaining, I will be on time for school and not consider Venice High a highly developed experiment in adolescent torture.

I try to imagine that my father will be drinking black coffee and reading a book at the kitchen table. He is sleepy-eyed behind his horn-rim glasses, smelling of the garden he tends each morning, about to go to work (this is before he lost his job and the depression and paranoia set in), looking like someone who could take care of anything, not let anything bad ever happen to his family. And that my brother will be there, with his hair standing up on the back of his head, his sturdy, tan little legs, and his dirty sneakers that get holes in them after just a few weeks. I will not complain that he has finished all the orange juice, is chirping songs like a bird, asking too many questions to which he already knows the answers—*Penelope, do you know how magnets work? Can you name a great African-American orator from the 1800s?*

What team scored the most home runs of all time?—or is wearing my basketball jersey. I will notice that his eyes are thoughtful gray like the sea at dawn, our mother's eyes.

But now all of this is as magical and far-fetched and strange as the myths my father once told me for bedtime stories. Shipwrecks and battles and witches and monsters and giants and gods are no more impossible than this.

Because, when I force myself to rise from my bed unbidden by anyone, and go downstairs, unbrushed, unanointed (my mother would not mind; it is safer this way in case any marauder should find me), the simple breakfast scene will not exist. The house will be broken and empty, the sea encroaching on the yard, the neighborhood flooded, the school—if I dared venture there—crumbled to scraps of barbed wire, brick, and stucco, the city named after angels now in hellish devastation as far as I can see. A basement full of canned goods and bottled water that my father provided, with more foresight than most, sustains me for another day that I do not wish to survive, except to await my family's return.

Fifty-three marks on the wall. If the world still existed, wouldn't someone have come by now?

Like the dead orchid beside my bed, I am still alone.

3

ANGELS OF THE
APOCALYPSE

NOEY HAD A JOKE *that we were going to start a band called Angels of the Apocalypse. I thought it was kind of stupid because only Noey could play anything—drums. Moira loved to sing and looked great doing it but she wasn't very good. It was a terrible band name anyway. Plus there were only three of us and as far as I knew there were four apocalyptic angels. But Noey had T-shirts printed with a photo of wings on the back and the name of the "band" on the front.*

She and Moira wore them to the Santa Monica Mall. I felt too embarrassed so I didn't wear mine.

While Moira tried on dresses I leaned over the railing and looked down at the people and stores below, imagining what it would be like to fall to one's death here. The mall, with its greasy smells and labyrinth of silver escalators leading nowhere, always made me hungry and tired like I needed something I could never have. I would rather have been home reading about the melting clocks of French surrealism or the dark, haggard faces of German expressionism.

This kid, Corey something, from our school was hanging out in the food court and he asked if we wanted to get high with him. I didn't, not because of the weed, which I actually liked the few times I'd tried it, but because I wanted to be with my friends, without the interruption. Corey was blond-banged and athletic-looking. Moira stroked her hair, coiling and uncoiling it around her fingers, while Corey sipped her soda and asked her to sing for him since she was in a band, after all, right? I almost cried and then pretended I had something in my eye, trying to concentrate on not letting my eyeliner run. We went to Corey's house and smoked in his living room until his mom came home and we escaped out the window.

"Such a hottie," Moira said later.

I looked at her lying on my bed with those freckles, that rose-colored hair, eyes of fractured jade, and something clenched in my stomach I didn't fully understand yet. I just knew I didn't want her to talk about this Corey person at all.

Noey sat cross-legged on the floor with her camera around her neck. She and Moira both liked being at my house more than their own (Moira's parents were always busy working; Noey's mom drank and yelled) so most nights my mom invited them for dinner. We helped her in the kitchen, making complicated paella, bouillabaisse, or lasagna with fresh herbs, meats, and produce from the Sunday Farmers' Market. Venice complained about too many girls being over but he looked at them with a kind of wide-eyed, starry-lashed wonder and they asked him about his latest obsession—baseball cards or video games or football season. My mother painted me and my friends as the three Botticelli Graces, dancing in a circle holding hands, almost exactly like the original, except for our blue jeans and cotton tank tops. Only Moira liked to pose but Noey and I did it anyway to please my mom. Besides, her paintings were amazing—as dreamy as they were lifelike—and we wondered if someday the painting of the three of us would be in a museum, keeping us together forever.

I knew eventually we'd be apart. I'd applied to study art history at NYU, Moira was going for fashion design at FIDM, and Noey had a scholarship in photography at Purdue.

Sometimes we had slumber parties in my room and I'd make up stories to help them sleep—tales based on the myths I'd read or the paintings I'd seen. Tales of the great heroes of the past, who sailed the seas, fought monsters, and rescued their friends and lovers. I made up words, too, which drove my friends crazy. ("Faunishness," Penelope? Really?) Sometimes I *made Odysseus, Aeneas, and Achilles into heroines instead. My friends liked that twist, although it wasn't always easy for me to do since the original stories were so male-oriented, the women in them often so passive or cruel.*

Moira, Noey, and I lay together, our long legs stretching out and entangling in our sleep. In the morning sunlight flitted through the trees, over their faces like a flock of butterflies, and I'd watch my friends while they dreamed, wondering if my stories were playing out inside their heads.

The butterfly is the first sign of life I've seen since the Earth Shaker. *Lepidoptera* is the scientific name. It sits on my windowsill, hardly moving its orange wings—veined with black like some elaborate stained glass. I want to look at it under a microscope, the horny proboscis and the tiny scales on the wings. My mother made collages with butterflies and had her own design of them tattooed across her back—four in various descending sizes to represent our family. I want this one to fly in here with me. The air outside is ashy and smells of smoke and rotting garbage. My room isn't much better but at least there is shelter. The solitary orchid my parents bought me on my sixteenth birthday is just a brittle stalk in a pot of dirt, but I bring it over to the window anyway.

The butterfly doesn't move.

"Are you dying?" I ask it.

I think it is dying.

Why are we here—just us and no one else? Is this salvation or the worst of punishments?

Today the butterfly is still alive, but a piece of its wing is missing. I'm sure it will die in a few minutes, an hour at the most, but later in the day it is still holding on. I wonder how it can be that tenacious; I would have given up long ago.

But maybe it has a reason to live, someone or something it needs to see.

I would wait forever to see my parents and Venice, Moira and Noey and Argos, but the chances of them coming back here are probably as slight as this butterfly growing a new wing and taking flight. Still, I am too afraid to leave and search for them.

Later that day the mutilated butterfly takes off into the gray sky and I wonder if it is trying to tell me something I'm not ready or willing to know.

4

THE MARAUDERS

IT'S BEEN SIXTY-EIGHT DAYS now and the hundred and twenty cans of food my disaster-conscious dad left for a family of four are more than half consumed, three quarters of the bottled water gone, in spite of my careful rationing.

The men come when I am sleeping. I wake to hear them outside in the darkness, shouting, laughing, and at first I think, *Someone is here! To save me!*

Then a voice shouts, "Overland's crib? Not bad. Weathered the fucking storm."

Overland! My dad.

"Noah's fucking ark. You think he's still in there?"

"Never know. If not, maybe the family. Heard the wife and daughter were hot."

"Any live female with legs would look hot to me just about now."

"You'd take anything with legs, man, live or dead."

"Fuck off."

I feel as I did in childhood nightmares where I became a Giant, my limbs tingling and thick and huge, paralyzed in my bed. There was a painting I found as a child, on one of my obsessive searches through my mom's art books; it was attributed to a follower of Francisco de Goya. *Colossus* had the stomach-tickling, skin-prickling allure of something I wasn't quite supposed to see, and showed a bearded Giant looming among storm clouds, above a scene of fleeing people and animals, his haunches turned to the observer and his head vanishing into blackness. That was what I became in my nightmares—the Giant. But I was not empowered by my size; I was dying from it.

And that is what I become again when I hear the men in the yard.

I can't move.

Pounding on the door. For a moment I wait for Argos to bark, my little-man dog that thinks he can protect me from everything. But he's gone, too. There's no one to protect me. My father filled the basement with all those cans of tuna fish, beans, anemically pale vegetables, and neon-bright fruit, all that water, but in spite of his talk about conspiracy and danger my mom never let him get a gun.

I heard my parents arguing about it more than once, after he lost his job—my dad saying we weren't safe, we needed protection, and my mom telling him he should see a psychiatrist. It *was* out of character for my dad, the idea of having a weapon. My parents were modern-day hippies, always believing in love and peace, never imagining a world where families and friends vanish, the sea eats the land, and men come in the night and pound on your door.

And break your windows.

The sound of glass shatters the spell of the Giant and makes me leap from my bed. Through the windows I can see shadowy, shambling figures in tattered clothes surrounding the house on two sides, standing on the strip of sand that isn't flooded with seawater; there is no way I am going to be able to get past them. In the mirror on my closet door, illuminated by the flashlights in the yard, is a pale, bony-faced, heavy-lidded girl with a flat chest, dirt smears on her cheeks and chin. Only her waist-length hair under her brother's old baseball cap gives her away.

I grab a pair of scissors in a plastic sheath—a weapon or a means to a disguise—and I head down the back staircase to the basement.

I notice that my hands are steady; they don't shake as I open the door with the key that I keep in the lock, and pocket it. My steady hands frighten me in a distant way, as if I am watching a movie and feel concern for the main character; her hands show not that she is brave but that she is not afraid to die, that she has already given up that much.

The basement is dark and smells musty and damp. Cans and bottles line the walls. My father's tool bench is here. He used it more and more after he lost his job at the lab, trying to take his mind off things. I think of him at work for hours, making dollhouses furnished with twig chairs and acorn tea sets—all of it so different from the scientific research he used to do. One house sits unfinished on the table. It is made out of bent willow with a thatched straw roof. So delicate. A big man could crush it in his hand.

I hear voices in the rooms above; the intruders are everywhere. Their feet pound on the floorboards. More glass shatters. A voice laughs so harshly it plunders the very air.

I am still holding the scissors, pointing away from

my body, as if I could hurt someone with them. Pathetic. I will not stab anyone with these. Although I might not be afraid to die, I realize I am afraid to fight. I remove my brother's baseball cap, take the blades to my own head instead, and hack away my hair.

In the dark basement I sit down on an old mattress and run my hands over my scalp. My head feels small and crushable—like a Giant's toy. I put Venice's cap back on.

Penelope Overland who had a loving father, mother, and brother, two best friends and a protective dog, a house and a city, but never quite felt safe? She's gone. Pen sits here on the mattress, staring into the dark, alone and even more stuffed full of fear.

It doesn't take long for them to find me. A light under the door frame. The door shakes on its hinges—the sound of a screwdriver in the lock—and it shudder-thumps open. I grip the scissor handles.

The man's sweatshirt is covered in grime and I can't see his face under the hood. His flashlight blinds me.

I just stare at him with the scissors held out in front of my body. Through the rest of the house I hear the other men stomping and yelling. It won't be long before more of them find their way down here. There's no other escape route except past the man's wide shoulders.

I need to run anyway. But where would I go?

"What's this?" he whispers, crouching and holding out his hand. "What do you have down here?" His flashlight moves from my face and scans the walls of the basement.

Shelves stocked with canned food, water. My supplies are dwindling. He and the other men will take everything. Who knows what else they'll take. Which one was he, yelling in the yard? *Heard the wife and daughter were hot.*

"It's mine," I say in my deepest voice. "You all need to leave." It sounds ridiculous, like I'm going to start crying.

He shakes his head and puts a finger to his lips. "It's not that simple. What's your name?"

"Get out of my house."

"Shhh, they'll hear." That's when he holds his flashlight up to his face and I see his eyes. Dark eyes like mine. He sets something down in front of me—it's a chocolate bar. I've eaten up the entire basement supply; it was my comfort the first few days, my only meal, and now they're all gone. I want chocolate; I remember reading somewhere that it can trick your body into feeling like it's in love. Sometimes when I looked at Moira I felt that way—a lightness, a tingling, an exhilaration mixed with calm. I still feel it sometimes when I dream of her, until I wake and remember that the world I knew has ended and everyone I have ever cared about is gone.

Not taking candy from strangers just doesn't seem to matter anymore so I reach out and point to the floor with the ends of the scissors, indicating that he should put the bar down, which he does. I grab it and shove it into my pocket.

"I had a kid," he says softly. "She fought constantly with her mother about the amount of sugar she was allowed to have."

I wonder why he's talking about this now. It seems so trivial.

The lines around the man's eyes deepen. "Where's your family?"

I just keep staring at him, trying not to think of their faces, smiling in a photograph under my pillow. (In the picture my mom is holding Venice and I have Argos on my lap in the same position, chest puffed out proudly because he's upright. My dad has his arms around all of us and is squinting just as proudly into the camera as if saying, "This is my wonderful family. Mine."—*Don't think of it now, Pen.*) I bite my lip and feel the little crescent moons of my teeth almost breaking the skin.

"Most everyone's dead."

"Everywhere?" I say. I didn't mean to reveal so much . . . what?—shock? vulnerability?—but it came out anyway.

"It could just be the U.S."

Just?

"Or more."

My stomach tumbles. Then why am I here? Why is he? I want to ask him but no sound comes out.

"You have to leave. They know you're here."

Who? Who are these men?

Something breaks upstairs. The big mirror above the mantelpiece? A glass-framed family photo or one of Mom's drawings? Or maybe it's the sound of my heart.

"Do you know how to drive?" the man asks.

I shake my head, no. I've only had a little practice and it didn't go so well.

"It may be time for a crash course. Not literally." It looks like he's trying to smile but his mouth just twitches. He holds out a cord with a key on it. "There's a van outside. Diesel. You can run it on vegetable oil. I can carry you out of here. You can take the van. It's stocked with food and water. We don't need any more blood on our hands."

"This is my house," I say. But I whisper this time. Following his command as if I trust him. At this point I know that screaming won't help me anyway.

"Why? Because you're here? Because your family owned it? No one owns shit now." His voice is harder.

"Why should I trust you?" I ask.

His eyes glance upward, toward where the other men are stamping and yelling. He spits into a corner of the basement. "Is there anyone else you know around here who you are going to trust?" Then he turns back to me and softens. "I started that yelling in the yard to warn you, if you were still here."

"Merk? You there? Found any fresh meat, man?"

Someone is coming.

The man, Merk, hisses, "I knew your parents, okay? You need to find them. There's a map in the van that might help. I can try to meet up with you later."

"You knew my parents?" *You need to find them....* "Where are they?"

"Look in the van. There's a map. I don't know for sure...."

This man, he could be anyone, a madman, eyes and promises glittering in my basement.

"Now let's get you the hell out." No more time for talk. He takes a large burlap sack and holds it over me—"Get in!"—but I jab at him with the scissors, grab the key from his hand, and run up the stairs.

The painting of me, Moira, and Noey as the Three Graces has fallen on the floor. Someone has slashed a knife through my canvas chest as if to steal my heart.

I fly past the big red-faced, lumbering zombie on the stairs. His cheeks bulge and squirm like there are live rats inside. I run through my house—where love once lived, and now death stalks with vermin—and outside into the gloom.

Ash swirls in the air and the landscape is gray rubble that falls away into the sea. They kept saying global warming wasn't going to be the end of us, that it was just threats from the fanatics, that we didn't have to make changes. But every year there were more earthquakes and floods and hurricanes and fires—every element expressing the earth's imbalance. Every year the temperatures soared and the ice melted and no one did anything. My pink house—no longer mine—stands on the edge of nowhere like a rose in a Salvador Dalí surrealist desert landscape. I stumble over what appears to be a neon-blue running shoe but as I kick it forward in the mud I see it's got something severed and human-looking inside. Somewhere in the back of my mind I remember a news story about the feet in shoes discovered on the coast off of British Columbia, the last one just last year—people thought it was a serial killer but they turned out to be the feet of the drowned whose insanely durable shoes refused to decompose.

Then I see a butterfly dart in front of my face; it's like the one that came to my window. It circles back and around my head, then flies forth to where a lime green VW bus is parked in the wasteland. I run toward the van, open the door, and scramble inside. Men are running out of the house, chasing me, howling. I jam the key into the ignition and turn it. The van jolts forward, careening over rubble and debris. Taking me away into this severed world.

Venice's cap is gone but I can't go back and look for it. That little soiled red cap he always wore, even to sleep. I touch my bare, bristling head remembering how his felt after he insisted on getting his floppy hair cut off every autumn and spring. He didn't like hair in his eyes but I thought he looked cuter, puppylike, with it long.

I sit in the van in the dark somewhere in this city behind a building with a caved roof, gnawing on the chocolate bar with my front teeth, thinking of Merk, the man who gave me the key. "I knew your parents," he'd said. How? Who was he? Why hadn't he just said that right away? "We don't need any more blood on our hands," he'd said. What did that mean? Is that what people did now, the ones who were left; did they go around killing people? I remember Merk's eyes. They reminded me of something. And he'd given me a car. Why? Because he knew my parents? He'd given me a candy bar and told me about his kid. My mom and I used to fight about sugar, too.

I take a bite of chocolate and close my eyes, seeing my mom's face. There are tears in her eyes.

When I was twelve I started being really mean to her. I couldn't help it; everything she did made me mad. Or, maybe it was just that she was the only person I could let my anger out at. One day I was running late for school and she asked if I had put on sunscreen. I said, "No, I'm late, leave me alone!" and she ordered me back.

I tried to push past her and she grabbed my arm and pointed to the bathroom.

"I'm late," I screamed again.

"It's not my fault. You're late because you ate too much sugar last night and didn't get up when I told you. . . ."

"You're such a bitch!"

She smacked me on the butt and I ran to the bathroom

sobbing, put on the sunscreen, and was twenty minutes late to school.

When I got home she looked like she'd been crying; her eyes were still puffy.

"I'm sorry," she said. It was the first time she'd ever hit me.

I mumbled I was sorry too. But I wouldn't let her hug or kiss me. It made me feel like I couldn't breathe. Like I was going to disappear, vanish back inside of her.

Two weeks later, on New Year's Eve, I was by myself in my room reading a biography of Frida Kahlo, while my mom and dad and Venice were downstairs watching a movie. When I went to the bathroom there was a small brown stain on my underwear and a red trickle in the toilet.

I asked my mom to come upstairs. "I think I have my period." My voice was soft; she didn't hear me at first. I had to repeat it, embarrassed even more because of how I'd been acting toward her. I was afraid she'd say, "My little girl is a woman now," or something stupid like that, but she controlled herself. Then I started to cry. "I'm sorry, Mommy."

"It's okay, love. I know. The way you're treating me, I don't love it. But it's pretty normal for your age. And especially with moms and daughters who've been really close."

(Even now, I can still hear her voice, as if she is in the van with me.)

"I missed you," I said.

"Me, too. I missed you so much."

The anger drained out of me like blood. We hugged each other, holding on tight. Like the world was going to end.

The chocolate bar is gone by the time I return from the memory; I haven't even enjoyed the dense crack of sweetness. As I lick the dark stains off my fingers I wonder if I'll ever know chocolate again, let alone the residue of love.

5

THE CYCLOPS

MANY OF THE ROADS are destroyed but I drive where I can, avoiding ditches and fallen, rotting palm, ficus, and sycamore trees, pretending that I know what I'm doing and thankful that at least the van isn't a stick shift. It doesn't really matter that I lurch and swerve along; there's no traffic. Maybe I'm going in circles; I don't know. The air outside the van is dark with soot and smoke, from the scattered fires, and beneath the burn is the sick-sweet smell of rot. There are no people to be seen. Live ones, anyway. I avoid the sight of the dead like I used to avoid the bad news on television. Back Then I read the *Encyclopaedia Britannica* or art history books, novels, or poetry but I have no books now when I really need them.

What I know is this: I have been sent on a journey. I was too afraid before, too afraid for over two months to venture out in the ruined spaces, even if it meant finding my family. But now I am on my way. Merk said he knew my parents, that I might be able to find them.

I've looked through the van for some kind of map but I can't find even that. Maybe Merk was crazy, but somehow I believe him, or at least I want to. He gave me the van, after all. And what if my family is somewhere out there? I let myself imagine it for a moment, let myself see their faces, see myself falling into their arms, safe in the house we make with our huddled bodies. We'll have one another. We can set up a camp, live out of the van, forage for food. It's all I want now. But I have no idea how much the world has changed, not only from the Earth Shaker but in the weeks after, no idea how I'll ever be brave enough to even find food and water, let alone fight whatever dangers exist.

We used to shop at this store a lot. Venice thought it was a big deal to go buy baseball cards and video games and plastic action figures when he was smaller. I always got mad at him for spending his money on overpriced stuff he'd grow tired of soon but

he never listened to me. But I was just as free with my allowance, buying underwear and socks, camisoles, slips, and pajama tops I'd wear with jeans during the day. My mom got rolls of toilet paper and cleaning supplies, bags of tea lights and the Christmas lights we strung up all year round. Strange, how exotic and dreamy that sounds now—a trip to the store for toilet paper with my once annoying, now wildly precious family.

The big red bull's-eye sign looms above the building. It's one of the few things still standing. There are huge cracks in the asphalt of the parking lot. I park the van and get out.

A gust of cold gray air bites at my neck, chest, and belly like a wild animal that knows where I am most vulnerable. Beads of moisture cling clammily to my skin. My legs shake from driving and from the cold.

Although the van is well stocked, I still have to find more vegetable oil fuel and more food and water, as well as personal supplies. I walk toward the glass doors where a thirty-foot fiberglass man in a sombrero stands guard. It looks like the burrito-stand man from Pacific Coast Highway. But how did he get here?

Something is piled in front of the store and I think at first it's more trash. But then I see these are bones—a heap of them. And there's no avoiding them now; I'm too close, without the protection of the van. I get that dizzy out-of-body sensation like I did when I was ten and we saw a dog hit by a car. Like it wasn't real. Though it heaved and bled black blood in the middle of the street, and my dad got out, wrapped it in a blanket, and took it to the vet where it died. I kept my eyes closed the whole way. And that was just one dog. There must be hundreds of bones here. Human bones. Gnawed raw. Just the hair left on the heads like string.

Through the smashed glass doors I see the aisles filled with things. Just things. But things matter now. They are all I am sure of. They will help me survive, drive, get toward something, anything. Get me away from this. So I keep my eyes open, still pretending the bones aren't real, go past them, and go inside.

The aisles are littered with dirt, the floors streaked dark in a way that almost seems obscene. Especially when combined with the fetid-flesh stench of the air. But the things still look pristine on their racks. Whoever came in here didn't get far. My footsteps echo on the linoleum where once, a million years ago, my mother rolled her shopping cart, baby Venice sitting inside pointing at the plastic toys.

I grab a cart and start to run, pulling things down off the shelves as fast as I can—alcohol and bandages and aspirin and tampons and toilet paper and sunblock and cans of food and bottles of water and vegetable oil. . . . Why hasn't the store been looted already? Does this have something to do with the pile of bones in front? Is someone lurking here? Guarding the supply? Ready to kill me? I must be quick and not think about any dangers.

I know this store well; I know where everything is and it's like I've been practicing for this moment for years, as if I knew, somehow, every time we shopped, that I'd have one last chance to grab the very last remnants of civilization from these shelves. Who is going to manufacture bandages and toilet paper now? Let alone electronics? Is anyone out there? Wouldn't someone besides Merk have come looking for me if they were? Is everyone in the whole world, besides me and Merk and those men who were with him, gone? If I once thought I knew heartbreak (the person I had a crush on only saw me as a friend, my dad had lost his job, and we thought we might lose the house, too), now I realize I had. Now I realize where the expression comes from. That area of my chest filled with fissures and erupted fault lines.

I remember the news stories about the terrible conditions of Chinese factories. All for the sake of our toys. But maybe China is okay; maybe people are still alive in

China, lined up in factories producing glittery little boxes full of light. Maybe there's a world beyond Los Angeles, or at least America, where everything is business as usual. But then why has no one come to my rescue? And why is the air so black and still?

And then, it isn't. Still.

The Giant of my dreams is here, standing above me.

Did he come out of the sea? Did he come out of the earth when it shook? Did he break the earth with his footsteps? Is he my hallucination?

He has to stoop to fit beneath the ceiling of the store. His skin is thick, warty, and pale. His forehead is high and furrowed. One eye socket is a ruined hole, sinking in on itself like a toothless mouth. The other eye rolls up, black and gelatinous and hungry.

This Giant reaches out and lifts me in his hand in just the same way as the figure in the Goya painting of Saturn eating his son, my legs and feet dangling straight down, my jeans pulling up, cutting into me, my rib cage crushed in huge fingers like it's a little basket woven of straw. Clammy flesh all around me. The store sways sickly below, my tiny shopping cart filled with pathetic-looking supplies. I think again of the bones at the door. I'm going to be part of that heap, my head ripped from my neck stem, my blood drained like wine, my flesh eaten away. I'm going to be bones at the end of the earth at the end of the world.

But I have something in my pocket, I have my scissors in their plastic container, and I pull them out and hold them up.

"What is your name?" His voice is thick with phlegm and the sulfuric smell from his maw makes me gag.

"Nobody," I say. I try to keep my voice calm, clear, strong but it sounds as compressed as my ribs feel. "Do you see Nobody?"

"I see Nobody," he says.

The room is tilting below and black dots swim in my eyes, half blinding me. "Do you harm Nobody?" I say.

"I harm Nobody."

The floor is far away. Will every bone in my body break if he drops me? What will that feel like? Venice broke his collarbone once just falling on the playground. I cried. I cried more than he did. Venice.

I don't see my whole life flashing before my eyes. What I see in my mind is my family in pain: my brother in a cast, my mother cooking more and more meals to try to make everything okay, my father on the phone with the bank after he'd lost his job at the lab. We never knew exactly what happened, only that it was

sudden, and that, before, he had been growing anxious, work-ing later every night. After, he changed. He became narrower-eyed, jumping at loud sounds. There was a year of fighting with the bank. "I just can't afford these rates on an under-water property. . . . You lost the paperwork again? I sent it three times. This is ridiculous. May I please speak to a manager?" Months and months of this. My parents arguing in their bed-room at night. My father saying there was a conspiracy, my mother begging him to seek counseling, medication. My mother crying. I was so afraid we'd lose our home and that maybe my father was losing his mind. Now I've had to leave the house and I wonder if my father was right after all. I think of the windows shattered, the paintings ripped from the walls as easily as ban-dages from a wound, the feather quilts torn apart. The man with the red face and cheeks full of dead rats. All that arguing with the bank came to nothing. They held my father in their palm, his legs dangling, a little nobody, and then everything was gone.

"I'm Nobody," I say again. "Child of Nobody. You don't see Nobody, you don't harm . . ."

And I close my eyes and strike out, strike the Giant in his one eye with my scissors.

There's a popping squelch sound and blood flies

everywhere. It's in my face, on my clothes, burning in my eyes, trying to seep into my mouth; I spit and vomit comes up.

He drops me, roaring. My body hits the linoleum floor.

I stagger and slide to my feet, still intact—though pain sears through me, hot as fire—lean onto the handle of my shopping cart for support, spin its wheels around, and run out of Hell's Eye, through the shards of cracked glass doors, past the heaps of bones. I, who was taught to hurt no one, not even to kill insects, to rescue and respect and protect all sentient beings, no matter how small. But what is sentient in this demon world? Nothing. Nobody. Nobody at all.

6

THE LOTUS HOTEL

VENICE USED TO HAVE nightmares about the world ending. I knew because I'd hear him cry out and I'd run to him. He'd be saying, "It's all our fault." Or, "The polar bear told me the ice would melt." Or, "The giants woke up and said 'No more!'" Once he told me he sometimes had to hide himself in his dreams, using his mind, so the dread monsters couldn't find him. It was hard work; he never felt really rested and there were dark rings under his eyes. Sometimes he peed in the bed and I'd hear his cries before my mom did. I'd strip off the sheets and help him change, and then he wanted to come into bed with me. He'd lie on his back with his knees bent up over my legs and I'd curl my arm around his waist and put my face against his neck. His skin was always so warm and soft except for the dried, dusty patches on his knees and elbows. His heart would beat faster than usual for a while, while I pressed the tender spot in the webbing between his first finger and thumb to relax him the way my mom taught me, and told him stories about boys who could magically make plants grow or repair the holes in the sky, until he calmed down and fell asleep.

I was wildly protective of Venice since the time he almost drowned. He knew how to swim then, but something had happened. When I surfaced from a dive, challenging him to do a better one, I saw that little body floating on the water, motionless. For a second I thought he was faking and then my heart was going to explode with terror and then I don't remember anything else. My parents told me that I pulled him out and gave him mouth to mouth which I had learned in a class once but thought I had forgotten.

Later, when he struck out in baseball, running off the field with his head scrunched into his chest, or when he was teased about being so smart, the teacher's pet, I remembered him floating in the pool, still as a dead flower, and wanted to sweep him up, away from harm. As if I had that power.

Venice never said exactly what he saw in the nightmares but he told me he was afraid the world was going to end. I told him it wasn't; I told him we were safe.

I drive as fast as I can away from the store from hell. I am stocked up with supplies I managed to dump into the back of the van before I tore away from the blinded Giant. Pain scorches when I move a certain way, and there is dried blood on my hands and on my thermal shirt. "We don't need any more blood on our hands," the man had said. I would rather be dead than part of a world like this. I keep thinking I'm going to throw up again, and my hands won't stop shaking no matter how hard I grip the steering wheel; it's like I have a violent fever that's trying to burn away the sickness of what I've seen and what I will become. I blinded someone. Something. I stabbed him. *It.* I pull over and open the door and vomit precious nutrients into the street.

Parts of the streets around the hotel are flooded with murky, mucked-up water. Who knows what lies under there? It rushes past me, black and frenetic. In the distance random fires, the only uneasy light, burn among piles of garbage.

I stay on the higher parts of the road. It's hard to know where I am because so much is gone. But I recognize the oddly shaped angular brick building standing like a Giant's slice of cake above the mire. An orange butterfly swoops past my windshield. I park and get out and limp after it toward the hotel.

My mom took us to the Culver Hotel to see the lobby with the milk-glass light fixtures and dark wood paneling, the velvet couches piled with brocade pillows. The actors who played the Munchkins stayed there when they filmed *The Wizard of Oz*. They swung from the chandeliers and fire escapes, my mom had said. Those crazy, drunken Munchkins. And we laughed. My mom loved this place. I can see her getting excited about an antique chair, a glass lampshade, as if she'd discovered some rare artifact. For her love of this place alone, I'll go inside; I'll brave whatever dangers. For what if she's somewhere here?

I put the van key around my neck and approach slowly now, hobbling, bruised from my fall. There will be blood-black wildflowers on my skin soon. My muscles feel like flayed meat wrapping my bones. It's dark. Candlelight reflects, flickering in the tall, curved leaded glass windows. Though I can no longer see the butterfly I walk toward this place. As if the orange wings have guided me here. As if I'll somehow find my mom inside.

I walk through the door.

The first thing I think when I enter is that the people

lying around on the couches in the candlelight have survived the Earth Shaker and do not have blood on their
hands, at least as far as I can see. Me, that's a different
story; I need a thousand showers to get this nasty, crusting
blood off of my skin and erase what I did.

The kids seem high, strewn out, half-naked, laughing. Some of them are crying, but in a luxuriant, dra-
matic way, as if from great happiness. No blood, but they
are all filthy. Cold wind rushes through some fracked-
glass panes carrying the smell of mildew and mud, with
something else—something sweet—woven in; the couches
are soaked with rainwater. The tall bookshelves are
empty. On one wall of the hotel is a huge painted mural
of a half-naked young woman sitting cross-legged on a
lotus flower. She is bright red, glowing ruby-ish, with
large gray eyes. Gray like my mother's, like my brother's.
I recognize her from my studies of mythology and religion as Tara, the Tibetan goddess of emptiness, action,
and compassion. She was born of the tears of empathy
from the eye of a bodhisattva. When she was a human
princess the monks told her she could be reborn as a man
but she chose the body of a woman as her vehicle of heal-
ing. The deity Tara comes in many colors but Red Tara is
the magnetizer of all good things, though I'm not sure I
believe that anything good exists.

"Hello, beautiful," someone says.

I turn and see a young man in black clothing. He has a shock of black hair and smoky green eyes. His body is slim and small but his shoulders are broad. There's a tattoo on his neck, inky writing I can't make out. I don't feel fear when I see him, only relief. He squints into my face. "How'd you get here?"

"Where's *here*?"

"The Lotus Hotel," he says. "See?" He points at something growing out of cracks in the marble floor. Large red flowers with layers of pointed petals sprouting like weeds everywhere. They're the first growing thing I've seen since the Earth Shaker. "Won't you have some, sparkle princess?"

He hands me a glass filled with red liquid.

I sniff. "What is it?"

"Punch!" He laughs. "I don't know. Something strong. We need something fucking strong, don't you think? The world actually *ended*. As in the *apocalypse*? We better have something strong."

"What happened?" I say. "It wasn't just an earthquake and a flood. Why is everyone gone?"

He shrugs. "Not everyone. Not us."

Why not us? I wonder. Why did I survive and why did he?

"And not the really big ones," he adds.

"What does that mean?" I think of the Giant with its poison white jellyfish eye.

"There are rumors about someone named Kronen who was doing this crazed top-secret genetic modification biowarfare in a warehouse downtown and some of his creations got released. They cracked the plates of the earth or some shit like that. They ate almost everyone."

"What?" I say, still seeing in my mind the gelatinous stuff oozing out of the Giant's socket. "He made them? You don't just *make* monsters."

"Who knows? You ever heard of that sheep they cloned?"

I nod; I had. My scientist father had showed me a video once. They took a cell from the mammary glands of one sheep, removed the nucleus and replaced it with the nucleus from another animal's cell, then implanted the hybrid cell in a third sheep that delivered it to term. Somatic cell nuclear transfer.

My father. I need to find him, I think, and almost say it out loud, but suddenly I'm so tired. And thirsty.

"What if someone cloned stem cells from a human who'd been genetically modified somehow?" The young man raises his glass to me and grins. "But don't worry yourself about that now. We're safe in here. Drink up."

He sounds like a charming madman but "charming" is the operative word and how long has it been since I've felt charmed? Plus I'm so, so thirsty. I can tell him about my family later. So I touch my lips to the liquid, the first fresh thing I've had in sixty-eight days. It stings a little, tightens and numbs like pomegranate seeds or persimmons or too much spinach. Already the smacking pain in my bones seems to lessen. And then I think, *This is all I want.* All I want is to forget what just happened with the Giant, forget what happened before that, stay here. To stay here getting high until I die. Free lotus potion and cute boys and girls sprawled around. All of it so easy, just for the taking. So what if it's a little cold; I have a thermal shirt and sweatpants. The dried blood on them doesn't matter anymore.

"Come on." He takes my hand   his is surprisingly small and I can feel the bones like twigs encased in flesh and we run through the lobby and up the staircase that swirls to hallways flanked by rows of rooms. The doors are all open and people are inside sleeping or hooking up, survivors like us. Broken bottles and clothing litter the hallways. A girl is crunched up into a ball, hugging her knees and whistling, pointing at the blank wall. Another is crushing red flowers so the juice drips into her mouth; some spills down her neck in rivulets. The young man takes me to a room with charred black curtains and a faint burned smell still in the air. The window overlooks the flooded streets below. It's so dark; any stars are masked in smoke and cloud.

"I love you," my new friend says. "What's your name?"

His name is Hex ("for Hexane," he says with a mellowish smile, "a hydrocarbon that is somewhat toxic but can cause euphoria and a somnolent state") but he doesn't remember how he got the name or the way in which he got here. None of the hotel dwellers seem to remember. They're here and that's enough. All day they pick the strange flowers that grow undaunted through the cracks, crushing the thick, wet petals in their hands and drinking the juice that pours forth into their cups. They seem to want to remain high all the time, hoping that the Earth Shaker was a bad trip and not willing to stop drinking and find out that they're wrong.

He takes off his black motorcycle boots, sits on the bed with the half-burned bedspread in the candlelit room he calls "Camp Hex," and gestures for me to join him. We watch each other over the tops of our glasses filled with the red drink. It may be toxic, radioactive, born of this ruined land but I don't care. It makes my throat burn and my eyes water and my mind bloom. Yes, bloom. Hex asks me where I come from, and I tell him about the one-eyed Giant and the man who gave me the van. I don't talk about my family because that already seems like a dream now; especially like a dream the more I sip. But I do say, "There's someone I am looking for."

"Everything you need is here, Pen."

I shake my head and look down at the bloodstains still on my hands. I want that shower. And food. But I don't want to go back out to the van.

I am already starting to forget who . . .

"I think there's a boy," I say. Very fast, very big eyes, lips that pout or easily spread into a smile that will need braces. What are braces?

Hex nods. His face is thin and pale, like his hands, with a few faded scars on his cheeks. "They're all gone," he says. "No use. Drink up."

I take another sip. The juice of the flower trickles down into my stomach, fills up my blood. I'm dizzy. All around the room are piles of books, Bibles, and magazines. I feel like maybe once I would have wanted to read everything but now I just stare at them.

"I collect any reading material I can find," Hex tells me. "Mostly from the shelves in the lobby. No one else seems to care. This is my prize possession." He shows me the book, pages stained and furled with water damage. *The Odyssey.*

"He used to read it to me as a bedtime story," I say.

"Who?"

But I can't remember. Somebody. Nobody?

"Everything is about the wine," says Hex, holding the book in his small hands, his thumbs jammed through holes in his big black sweater. "The sea, the wine, hospitality, loyalty, courage, *kleos.* Meaning glory. What would your book be about?"

"The pink house at the edge of the sea," I say, even though I don't know what that means. "The Giants, the blood, the eyes, the butterflies."

For some reason the word "butterfly" makes me look again at the words tattooed on his neck. "Hey, what does it say?"

"*Non sum qualis eram.* I am not what I once was."

"Cool."

"It's from a book I love."

"Are you?"

"What?"

"What you once were."

"I can't remember."

We giggle, little bursts of fireworks in my solar plexus.

"Maybe some of these items will spark your memory," he says, gesturing around the room.

I wander about, looking at his collection—batteries, paper clips, pencils, nails, a nail file. There is a cell phone and I hold it up to punch in some numbers that somehow seem important but nothing happens.

"I like to tinker with electronics, take things apart and put them together again. It's how I relax." He grins at me. He has little fangs—tiny vampire teeth—and lips pink as lip gloss.

Next he picks up a globe of the world and spins it so the pale colors blur. I want to cradle it in my arms. I can see a room filled with maps, the walls papered with maps in the same soft colors as the ones on the globe, the vast pale blue oceans, the jagged landmasses, created by ancient movements of the earth. But where was that room? And what has happened to all that land?

"I wonder if it's still even here," Hex says, as if reading my mind. "Maybe it's just us in the Lotus Hotel."

Through the fractured glass window an orange butterfly darts, landing for a second on Hex's wrist before flying away. We both blink at it like it's a hallucination.

"I have another one," he says.

"Another one what?"

He holds out his arm and pushes up his sleeve.

Another tattoo—the word *Faithless*—is inked blackly against his pale skin.

He might be faithless but I believe in him. I think he's an alchemist, like one of the elongated, androgynous figures from a Spanish surrealist painting I think I used to love (or did I dream it?), a creature living in a distorted tower with black and white parquet floors, caring for a wan-faced, trapped moon. Hex reads *The Odyssey* aloud to me.

> " '*But any of . . .* [*my men*] *who ate the honey-sweet fruit of lotus was unwilling to take any message back, or to go away, but they wanted to stay there with the lotus-eating people, feeding on lotus and forget the way home.*' "

Forget the way home. A mild worry nags at me but it's so slight, like when you've left the house and think you've forgotten to turn off the stove but you know you really have so you don't go back (should you?). Then Hex begins to hum song after song I vaguely remember—something about being loved until the world comes to an end—and I slump against him, forgetting the unattended imaginary flame on the imaginary stove. His sweater is so soft, I think, as I fall asleep on his bed. Sheets that smell of smoke and old books and of him.

7

BULL'S BROTHER

WE STAY HERE FOR DAYS, I'm not sure how many—I've ceased my counting. Once I made red marks on a wall. Here the only red marks are the ones on my body, but they've turned black and purple by now. We drink the juice of the impossibly alive red flowers we pick from the cracks in the lobby floor and they make our mouths pucker and stain our tongues bright red, soothe our souls. Sometimes one of the boys or girls from the hotel comes into our room and sits on the bed with us, cross-legged, long hair streaming down slender shoulders. Sometimes they kiss Hex on the lips and a part of me wonders if it would bother me if I wasn't so high.

"Who are you?" I ask a girl in a tattered black silk slip. Her eyes are so pale and murky they look blind, or maybe visionary.

She leans over and digs her ragged nails into my arm so I pull back. "The elves of the Lotus Hotel. We came from underground."

For some reason this makes perfect sense to me. "Why did we all survive the Earth Shaker? And no one else," I ask.

"Oh, we are special," she says. "Chosen. Of the clan of earth, water, fire, or air. I stopped a fire myself, just like him."

She kisses Hex's lips and leaves. He leans over and rests his head on my shoulder, gazing at the ceiling; I stroke his coarse black hair.

"What fire?"

"I'm kind of a slut," he says, ignoring my question. "I confess I manipulate people with my sex-charm. It's for survival. I'm sorry."

Nothing seems to bother me. I smile again and run my hands over the peeling, flocked wallpaper. Little velvet leaves and flowers, a pattern that I try to analyze to see where it repeats, though it's hard to tell. You could go crazy trying! I think, and laugh out loud.

The girl comes back holding a guitar. She gives it to

Hex and leaves again. I notice she is wearing running shoes with her slip dress and I almost remember something I don't want to and wonder if the shoes will ever decompose.

Hex takes the guitar in his hands like a baby and runs his fingers over the strings. Then he plays for me. It's a song that sounds vaguely familiar but I don't know for sure. His voice is rough, but soothing.

"It's funny to substitute the word 'squirrel' for 'girl' in pop songs," he says. "Also, 'hams' for 'hands.' Like 'I kissed a squirrel, and I liked it.' Or 'Put your hams in the air.' Want to try? It's fun."

"I don't think I remember any songs," I say.

" 'Sexy' is *always* 'Hexy.' 'I'm hexy and I know it!' Try it, Pen!"

I laugh, his voice tickling my neck like fingers.

" 'Baby' is 'rabies.' 'Young' is 'dumb.' 'You' is p . . ."

"Okay, I get it, I get it."

"What about apocalypse songs? My specialty. I have a whole set list. 'Blood Sport—Sneaker Pimps.' 'Smoke and Mirrors—RJD2.' 'Ambulance—TV on the Radio.' Oh, and this is old school . . ." He strums the guitar hard and sings in a deep voice, " 'This is the end, my friend.' "

The words make my spine as cold as his voice is hot. "Is it safe here?" I say.

That's when the room shakes and even the warm high is penetrated with the kind of dread that numbs you cold and I think, *Another Earth Shaker,* but it's not. Not that kind. Or maybe they are the same. Hex said something about Giants cracking the plates in the earth.

Someone screams downstairs and we peek out into the hallway, Hex's hands on my shoulders. Kids are running up the staircase. We go to the top of the stairs. A huge something hulks in the lobby. It hits the milk-glass light fixtures so they sway over the rubble and water and lotus flowers.

"Who blinded Bull?" the thing wails. "Who blinded my brother?" Its voice sounds like an ambulance siren but deeper.

Bull's brother. The massive creature picks up a candelabra and waves it around the room. Turning everything to a black-and-white horror show flickering on a movie screen.

"It's one of Kronen's," Hex says, as the Giant holds the candelabra up to the torn drapes. Almost instantly they become flames themselves, the whole room a red velvet conflagration.

Hex shoulders a black leather backpack adorned with zippers like a motorcycle jacket, and we take the fire escape—iron stairs scaling the side of the building—and swing off the last rung onto the cracked pavement below.

We hear screams from the hotel, glass breaking.

A sudden gust of wind carries the fire from the brick building out into the courtyard, dead trees igniting. A pile of wooden beams in the street catches, blistering with red sparks, blocking us from the van. Smoke blinds and chokes me.

Hex takes my hand. It's hard to see but it looks like he's holding his other palm out toward the flames, muttering something. Instantly they subside. What did he do? Was there a fire extinguisher?

We run to the van, unsteady. Half-drunk. My eyes and throat still stinging. How can I drive like this? Hex grabs the key from my hand. Not that he could walk a straight line either. *Don't Drink and Drive* warnings flash like neon in front of my eyes but back Then you didn't have to escape man-eating Giants. Like we do now.

"Let's go," Hex says as if to himself—he's driving. "Go go go."

Earthquake. Flood. Fire. Giant cannibals.

We go.

8

THE SIRENS OF BEVERLY HILLS

HEX AND I DRIVE NORTH and then west according to the compass he keeps in his pocket. The only reason we chose this course was because the road was less ruined and we were able to make our way slowly through the rubble and flooding.

I can still taste the lotus juice in my mouth, making my tongue furl up, sore with longing for more. *I'm so thirsty.* There's still water in the van (thankfully no one broke in and stole it while I was on my lotus bender) but Hex doesn't have any bottles of the potion with him.

"It'll force me to sober up," he says. I don't know why he'd want to, but I refrain from saying so.

"The Giant won't get far," he continues, almost cheerfully, as he drives. "Either he'll burn in the fire or drink some wine and be out for a few days."

After he eats them, I think. *The ones who didn't burn to death. Fire clan or no.*

Hex eyes me sideways where I sit in the passenger seat with my feet tucked up under me, winding a length of coarse rope, that was among the supplies in the van, around my hands. I still haven't washed off the Giant's blood.

"He is after you, right? He said something about his brother."

I shrug and shiver myself into a smaller ball. My high is wearing off fast.

"I thought so. You blinded Kronen's Giant, homegirl? That's impressive."

"I don't know," I mumble.

"The Cyclops!" Hex reaches into his backpack and pulls out the book, points to it as he quotes:

"'. . . he . . . caught up two together and slapped them, like killing puppies, . . . and the brains ran all over the floor, soaking the ground. Then he cut them up limb by limb and got supper ready.'"

I try to shiver off the image.

"Why the hell are there *Giants*?"

"Kronen cloned stem cell–manipulated beings, somehow enhanced so their bones wouldn't break from the strain of the size?" Hex wonders aloud. "Maybe it was funded by some secret corporation, to gain power? Or maybe the Giants were the last straw that caused the earthquake that ended the world? I have no idea."

"Where are we going?" I ask, hoping he has a more lucid answer for this question than for my first one.

He shrugs. When we stop it's because we have to. A large expanse of swampy water stretches out in front of us. And we hear singing.

Not just any singing—it's high-pitched, too high, eerie but gorgeous. The words don't make any sense but I want to catch them, rearrange them into something my mind understands. *Hey ho the runway in the blimey blithely air! Shooting sugar into your lines and crevices. Say chic luxe fortitude be-glistens your wrecked eyeballs' celebrity against the sea storm of my heart. Lachrymose! Oh you will be smote with bows and trinkets of botulism oblivion, birthday girl!* Hex stops the van and gets out and runs to the edge of the swamp. I follow him. For some reason I bring with me the coil of rope. My companion crouches and stretches out his hand toward the water.

The air sweats sulfur, rank in my nostrils.

A head emerges, then another. Girls. Their hair is

long and tangled, thick with mud, their noses small for their faces. They rise up and we see their bare breasts and emaciated torsos. They are wearing jewels, all kinds of necklaces and bracelets and rings coated with mud and entangled with weeds. Around them in the water float shoes and more jewels and mannequins in what were once expensive items of clothing.

"Come to us," the girls sing. "He won't smell you here, in the mud. Giants can smell you out good, you remember? 'Fee Fi Fo Fum.'"

This part of town, it's familiar but so changed. The palm trees have fallen, necks snapped like slaughtered birds'. The buildings have crumbled, large sheet glass in piles of shards. This is where the wealthy once roamed in their shiny cars. A leviathan of a Rolls-Royce lies busted and belly up at the edge of the swamp. Not a butterfly in sight. I'm starting to imagine them as guides and I don't think they want me to be here.

"Come on," Hex says to me but I pull him back.

"We have to go," I say.

"They're so pretty." He sounds high again, gazing at the mud-slicked bevy of girls, and my stomach ties itself into a perfect bow.

One of the girls turns her head and smiles at me, heart-shaped lips baring large teeth. Her hair is matted with black oil and her cheekbones are sharp enough to do damage. "I used to love pretty things," she whisper-hisses, slithering toward us, her bony back arching from the mud. "Wicked jewels and shoes. I went shopping all the time. Attended the showings of the hottest collections. Had the best plastic surgeons in town remake my entire face and body as if from scratch. But it was never enough." She flings her head from side to side, strings of hair streaming out, flicking mud. "Now I can have whatever I want. Come into the swamplands of Beverly Hills where all the jewels are free and there are no men to worry about impressing." She grins at Hex. "Except you! Lovely boy!"

I tighten my grip on his arm.

"Isn't it major?" The swamp creature holds something up out of the dark ooze. It's not a boho-chic paisley dress or a lavender-and-black tweed suit draped with chains or a nude-and-black lace blouse, all of which I might recognize as "major" from Moira's leftover magazines.

It's a human skull.

Hex leans closer to look at it. The girl reaches out her hand and grabs at his sweater, lifting herself up out of the water. "Now you are a man to keep!" Her breasts are fake-looking and her waist is disproportionately small.

"Hex!" I say. "No!"

I pull at him and fall backward onto the muddy ground. He stops and looks at me.

"Pen?"

"We have to go," I say, struggling to stand, slipping. "Please. You'll die there. Remember the sirens luring the men to their death?"

"Yes. The book."

"Stories," I say. "I'll tell you a story. Come on."

He looks at me, then back at the girl with the skull. Something glitters grimly in its eye sockets. Something that princesses and movie stars would have worn on their fingers.

"The sirens," Hex says. He sits down in the mud beside me, still watching the girl. "I have always been a sucker for pretty girls. Especially ones who can sing. Even mean ones. I'd do anything for a pretty girl."

I take the rope I'm still carrying and wrap it around his wrists, tie it in a knot the way Venice learned in Cub Scouts. Hex lets me do this without even flinching, as if he doesn't know I'm here.

"Come on," I say, standing, tugging. He doesn't weigh that much more than I do so I'm able to get him to his feet. "I'll tell you a story."

I drive as far away as I can get from the swamp. Hex is in the passenger seat, the rope still around his wrists. He keeps looking out the window and moaning softly. I start talking, telling him the first thing that comes to my mind, a memory from before the Earth Shaker:

Moira and Noey in a pool . . . ? The last time I saw them and it was only an image on my computer.

"Gavin's having a Christmas party," Moira said, brushing her hair. She insisted we call her Ginger and it was accurate anyway; her hair was a blush color more than an actual red.

I could feel my jaw tighten. I don't want to go.

"Come on, Penelope." Noey had noticed my reaction; she knew me so well. "We need to get you out of here."

They didn't think it was healthy that I avoided leaving my house if I could help it, but what was the point of going any-where, especially if they were there with me?

"You guys go. There's some reading I want to catch up on." It wasn't an excuse; I had a date with Ovid.

"Oh shit, Penelope." Moira came and sat beside me on the bed. She had tried semi-successfully to cover up her freckles with makeup but I loved the way they played across her face. "You need to live a little."

For me, living was that, being there with them, but they didn't understand. They told me I wasn't active enough. Not that they were exactly action heroes but they sometimes went to political protests; I didn't like the crowds. Noey took tae kwon do and Moira rode horses and surfed. I was weak and awkward, barely passing PE most years. Noey took photographs of Moira she called "girlist," partial body shots of long legs in torn stockings and violently high, toe-crushing shoes, torsos in bathtubs with rose petals that looked like blood, hands squeezing a tiny roll of belly fat, eyes dripping mascara. The pictures made a statement about our female dissatisfaction. My reading and studying and retellings of old stories didn't do anything except help me think better. I was at least thoughtful. Too thoughtful, my friends said. And all I thought about was myths and old paintings that made me feel drunk on wine or struck by lightning but didn't matter to most people.

Let's take some photos at the beach. There's a party on the boardwalk. There's a housing protest downtown. Close your books. Come dancing. Come swimming.

I had no outlet, my friends said, no place to let out my frustration and anger at the world except the occasional fight with my mom. But Noey said yelling wasn't taking action; it was desperation and it didn't change things.

"It just makes your throat hurt and raises your blood pressure. That's the only way my mother feels she can control her life and it sucks," she said.

Noey and Moira weren't close to their parents like I was. Noey went to AL-ANON meetings to deal with her mother's alcoholism and Moira's therapist thought her mom was a narcissist. Mostly they just avoided their families, retreating to my house when they needed some parental affection and a good home-cooked meal. But after dinner with us that night, Moira and Noey ended up going to Gavin's party. I watched them from my window as they ran across the lawn. Moira in a faded pink denim miniskirt and a light green lace T-shirt and Noey in purple skinny jeans and a black hoodie with small silver stars on the back. They were laughing and their hair was shining like leaves in moonlight, their limbs long as saplings. I thought, Girls are magical at this phase, girls are invincible, nothing can touch them. I didn't think "us" because I didn't feel that; I felt other, on the outside, watching them. I stayed at home with Ovid's Metamorphosis. At least I was smart, I told myself. I read the encyclopedia for fun. Not everyone could do that. Would want to do that, my friends would have said.

Noey texted me Sally Mann–esque photos of Moira's legs in tie-dyed stockings dancing, Moira's hair flying out across her face, under a halo of red and green heavy glass Christmas lights, Moira's bare belly with a boy's hand grabbing her belt. The last one was of Noey's legs dangling in the water while Moira kissed a boy, both of their heads emerging above the misty pool, her hair afloat around them. She looked like a siren, who could lure him to his death if she chose.

I went to sleep staring at the last image, wondering, not what his mouth tasted like, but hers.

This part, this last, I don't tell Hex, although I trust him enough to tell him anything—don't I?—so I'm not sure why I don't. Because I don't want him to know I had a crush on a girl or because I have a crush on him? He's asleep anyway, though, and my eyelids are dropping shut over my eyes like the lids are forged of silver, so I stop the van and untie the rope from his wrists. Maybe it's not the best idea for us both to sleep at the same time but it's better than crashing the van. It's dawn and the air is a silty gray. I hope the cloud cover will hide us from danger. If I let myself, I'd be able to hear the girls singing in the distance, wanting us back, like the sirens in the weirdly prophetic book that lies on the seat between me and Hex. The book scares me a little now but I pick it up anyway.

"You will come first of all to the Sirens, who are enchanters of all mankind and whoever comes their way; and that man who unsuspecting approaches them, and listens to the Sirens singing, has no prospect of coming home."

9

BEATRIX THE WITCH

SLUMPED IN THE DRIVER'S SEAT of the van I have a dream I've had versions of before:

Venice doesn't come home from school. I ask my mom where he is and she says she let him walk alone. I scream at her and call a phone number. Venice answers, says he is with a friend and I ask him to put the friend on. It's a man who laughs and tells me that his daughter and Venice are in class together. I ask the daughter's name and the man hangs up. When I call back, his voice is deep and hollow, and when I ask to speak to Venice— Please, please put him on—he keeps laughing and saying, "Who? Italy? Rome? Who do you want to speak with?" I am screaming and tearing at my mom's clothes, begging her to go find Venice, but she keeps cleaning the house. I have a large cut on my knee that is deepening into a bloody hole. There is a gypsy fortune-teller sitting in a balloon-festooned cupola on a hill in a park. She asks me if she can read my fortune but I run away screaming, stepping in piles of dog shit, searching for my brother. . . .

When I wake up my whole body hurts, like poison has been injected into my veins. I wonder if the planet feels like this after everything we've put her through.

Someone is stroking my head with hands gentle as my mom's. For a moment I wonder if she will be there beside me. . . . My chest tightens with hope.

It's Hex, sitting up in the passenger seat. He doesn't ask me what the dream was and I'm grateful. Not that waking up is much better. Except that he's here.

"Are you okay?" he asks. His voice sounds the clearest I've ever heard it. The lotus potion must have completely worn off.

"I had a dream. About my brother."

"You want to tell me?"

So I do. I tell Hex about my family, how we were separated, how I was afraid to go out looking for them, how Merk came and sent me on the journey, how the

Lotus Hotel waylaid me, how I have to keep looking though I have no clues.

"I'll help you," he says. "If I can." He looks away and swipes a hand across his eyes. "I had a dream, too. About those kids at the hotel. I was too fucked up to realize. What must have happened to them . . ." He swallows like he's trying to push something large and bitter back down his throat.

"I'm sorry," I say. I think, *I want to help you, too,* but I don't tell him because what could I do to help anyway? I'm pretty sure those kids are all dead by now.

My stomach growls then, so loud it's like there's an animal in the van with us. Hex smiles, as if glad for the distraction, though I'm embarrassed by the insistent sound of my hunger. "We'd better feed you, right?"

I get a whiff of myself as I sit up. I'm covered in dried mud, which is preferable to Giant's blood, I guess, but not much. "Starving and stinking."

"S and s. At least we're sober now."

"That was quite a high."

He frowns and pats his pockets like he's searching for a cigarette. "I guess I just wrecked eighteen months of sobriety, but does lotus juice count?"

"Do you not want it to?"

"It counts. I was fucked up for . . . how long?"

We figure I was at the Lotus Hotel for about two weeks and if I add that to the time I counted on the wall of the pink house it's been almost three months since the Earth Shaker.

Hex tells me that back Then, when he was twelve, he started drinking and using, doing whatever it took to get his supply. "Good times." At thirteen he was a full-blown addict and it got worse when he started DJing five years later because he could get into all the clubs and everyone was always giving him free alcohol and drugs. "I was like this mini–pill machine, downing them with whiskey. Could drink a dude twice my size under the table." When his best friend Yxta died from an overdose, he dragged himself to a meeting and quit cold turkey. Until the end of the world.

As he speaks I see a picture in my mind, as if I'm looking at one of the old master paintings I love. It's a child, very small, sitting in a room frowning into a mirror. Sunlight dapples the pink walls. I want to take the child in my arms.

"But it doesn't really matter now if I'm sober or not, does it?" Hex says, snapping me out of the vision I don't understand.

It does matter, I realize, now that the lotus-juice high has fully worn off; it's the only way we will be able to really survive this journey. But I don't want to upset him for "going back out," as he calls it, and I can tell, by the shade he's pulled down behind his eyes and the way his jaw twitches when I start to ask, that he doesn't want to talk about the friend who died or why he got high at twelve in the first place. "I think we can start fresh now," I say gently. "We need our wits about us."

"'Wits about us'?" He purses his lips and shakes his shoulders, teasing. I'm glad that at least he can still tease me right now. "Are you from another century?"

"Sometimes I think so. But you're the one who's always reading from Homer."

"Point taken. But we need food as well as wits. Dig in." He holds up a can of chili and a bag of chips from our stash in the car.

"Sounds blissiant."

"What?"

"I make up words sometimes. It means 'divine.'"

He laughs. "Okay then."

We eat the cold beans and stale chips and then use up some of our precious water for very much needed sponge baths in the back of the van. Hex keeps his undershirt and boxers on and turns away, hunching his bone-thin shoulders as he washes himself. The knobs of his spine are clearly visible. I'm surprised that, despite his bravado, he's even more modest than I am. Maybe because he's not high now. My curiosity about him keeps me from worrying about what he thinks of my own skinny, bruise-marred body.

He puts on a clean black T-shirt and jeans from his leather backpack and a pair of black high-top basketball shoes with gold trim. I eye the clothes, jealously, I guess, because he offers me an extra T-shirt and jeans from the same pack. Or maybe he just can't stand to see me in my blood-mud-crusted thermal and sweats anymore?

"Do you only wear black?" I ask him.

"Yep. Sorry you don't get much selection." He tosses me the empty backpack. "This isn't exactly a department store."

"Are you kidding? I meant, thank you. Fresh clothes are the best thing in the world."

"Besides metal-flavored canned beans."

"Mmmmm."

I scrape out the can for the last remnants and set it aside in a box. He asks what I'm doing.

"Recycling?"

"Is there much point?" Hex asks.

It's just a habit, I guess. "Maybe we'll be able to use them for something." The piles of garbage everywhere don't need to get any bigger. "Maybe it still matters."

"That's what I like to see." He taps the inside of his forearm where the tattoo is and then covers the last four letters so it reads *Faith*. "Someone needs to have some."

Not that I think I really do but I can at least pretend.

Maybe just driving is some form of faith, rather than giving up, curling up in a corner of the van, and waiting to die.

"Wait," I say. "There's somewhere around here I want to go."

Hex stops the van in front of a crumbled mansion with an ornate metal gate. It hangs on its hinges, swinging in a gust of wind that chills me like cold iron on the nape of my neck. The only reason I'm not too afraid to go in is that I glimpse the orange butterfly for a moment, before it vanishes, consumed by shadow.

We enter through the gate and walk up a winding path that leads to ruined stone steps. In the front courtyard is a round fountain basin full of stagnant water. Broken light fixtures survey us like shattered eyes.

"Greystone Mansion," I say. This is the historical, supposedly haunted Doheny mansion. My mother took me here when I was young to see the architecture, as wonder-filled as if she were ushering me inside the pages of a book of fairy tales. That's why I want to go here now. *She was here. We were here together.* But the place seems so different without a world around it.

We go through the enormous arched doorway into an entry hall. The gray roof has caved in and dead trees curve like praying hands over the top of the house. Someone has hung broken crystal chandeliers from their branches. Piles of dried leaves cover the cracked black-and-white tiled floor. I recite to myself what I've memorized of the parts of plants listed in the encyclopedia—*guard cell, upper epidermis, waxy cuticle, stoma, palisade mesophyll, spongy mesophyll, vein, waxy cuticle, lower epidermis*—like an incantation to return the flora to life. At the back of the room is a massive mound of broken statuary and furniture, branches, rocks, jewelry, electronics, and books. There are lots of cracked carved stone plaques depicting obscenely old-mannish-looking, screaming babies straddling piles of fruit.

There's a woman, stretched languidly on a leather couch with lion-carved feet, her black hair falling over her breasts. She wears a sheer, one-shouldered dress, the same lilac color as her eyes and as the disintegrating dried flowers scattered on the floor. Her skin is very white and you can see the lilac-blue veins running through her.

I think of a painting from the Pre-Raphaelite period,

a Waterhouse painting maybe, so sweet and pretty but so throbbingly sexual at the same time.

A young man crouches on the floor staring at the woman and sketching furiously on a tablet. Beside him is a large, three-tiered cake—green frosting roses on top—that he stuffs into his mouth as he sketches. There is cake on his face and in his curly red hair.

"Who are you?" she asks, waving her hand at us, raising her defiant chin; she has the chiseled, symmetrical bone structure of a mannequin.

"Pen and Hex."

"You sound like a Las Vegas act. And in your matching clothes!" She snickers. "This is Ez." She points at the young man. "He's mine."

He blinks up at us. His eyes like Venice's when he played video games for too many hours. But these eyes aren't gray; they're deep brown, almost amber. He's wearing a large dog collar around his neck and attached to the collar is a leash that the woman holds in her hand. There's an orange butterfly perched among his curls, fanning its wings like a lady cooling herself down at a fancy dress ball.

"Aren't you . . . I knew it! You're her, aren't you?" Hex says to the woman in lilac.

I look at him, trying to figure out what he's doing.

Then I see the huge TV with the photo of the woman and a tall, dark-haired man taped to the screen.

She smiles, a bittersweet twist to her lips. "I was her. If a soap opera star falls in a house and no one is there to see, does it mean she isn't there?" She laughs in a strained way and lights the cigarette that's been dangling loosely, as if forgotten, from her fingers.

Hex picks up a butt from the floor. "Do you mind if I keep this as a souvenir?" There's red on the tip. "It touched your lips."

"Silly boy. You want one? Just one." She holds out another cigarette and he comes toward her, reaches for it. But she holds on just a little too long and I realize I want him to move away from her. Instead, as she lights the cigarette he bends even closer so their hands are almost touching.

I've never seen him smoke but he does it naturally, hungrily, closing his eyes, almost shivering with relief, like he's been dreaming of this moment since the Earth Shaker. The smoke makes me cough and he quickly aims it away from me and hunches back a step. "So you're really her."

"Beatrix Ray," she says. "And you have come to my world. This is Ez and he is my minion. Thus you will be." She holds out two leather dog collars.

Collars.

I notice Hex's small but well-defined biceps flinch. "We really should be going," he says.

The woman picks up a silver bell shaped like a lily and holds it in the air, then rings it. We feel the building shake as if the bell caused this and I turn to Hex. That sound, that rumbling, means run. But we can't.

"Frakk," Beatrix says. "These are our new friends. See that they are properly kept."

The Giant's feet are thick, bare, and bloated like those waterlogged corpses I once saw in the street in front of the pink house. The feet send more cracks through the tiled floor where he steps, like hammers. When I try to look at him black particles float dizzily through my eyes so I keep my gaze on the ground. But when I finally glance back up I see that he's wearing a crude, garish pink papier-mâché mask in the shape of a pig's head. That he's caught the butterfly perched on Ez's head. And crushed it between massive fingers.

Hex takes my hand and leads me toward the woman. I remember his words, *I'd do anything for a pretty girl.* I reflexively pull back but he squeezes my fingers and catches my eye.

Conveying: *It's okay. Trust me.*

"Ez," she says. "Collar them."

He lowers his eyes and won't turn his face to her. She jerks the leash attached to his collar and he makes a small sound and stumbles forward. With the Giant watching us (for I feel his eyes, though I won't look) we kneel, letting Ez put the collars with leashes around our necks and then fasten them to a marble post. The moldy collar pinches the skin of my throat and I swallow against it, suddenly afraid I won't be able to breathe.

"May we have a place to sleep?" Hex asks. "Please. We're very tired." He can be as charming as a little girl when he wants to be.

"But first you must eat." The woman opens a curtain and gestures to a banquet table piled with multicolored cakes and other pastries. "Even my minions eat. Isn't that right, Frakk?"

I hear a sound, like the echo of a hollow building collapsing, coming from the Giant's throat.

"No, no, they're not your dinner. Have some cake," Beatrix tells him. "And you, too, Pen and Hex."

Hex catches my eye and shakes his head no so slightly I'm not sure if I actually saw it.

"Oh thank you, Beatrix. We're not hungry now. But we would love to be able to rest a little."

"First you must hear my story," she says. "Frakk likes it, too." She whispers to us, "It's how I bewitched him."

I look at Ez, still stuffing his face with frosting, and think of Odysseus's men, turned into pigs by the witch, Circe. *The Odyssey* is our guide. Maybe that's why Hex signaled that I shouldn't accept the cake.

Hex sits at Beatrix's feet and gestures for me to sit behind him. I want to lean my head on his shoulder but not as much as I want to get out of here. I have a feeling that's what he's going for, in spite of the huge monster obstructing the entrance.

"I've lost my true love," she says. "Not to mention my career. I was once queen of the air." She points to the broken TV and the photo of her and the man. "That's me with my co-star and real-life lover. But everything changed so I was prepared for the apocalypse. I became a practitioner of dark arts just in time and now I will reign over the ruin!"

She goes on and on like this, smoking and talking in an affected voice that sometimes wavers into a pinched British accent. She tells us of lost lovers, starring roles, premieres, gowns, feuds, and her worldwide pursuit of spells to keep herself young forever. The Giant hovers near the door, blocking with his girth what remains of the fading light. Ez sketches and stuffs his face with cake. Finally both he and Beatrix fall asleep and the Giant turns his head to watch us. I've made myself actually look at him straight on—he's rocking back and forth and waving his hands around the pig mask over and over again.

"How are we going to get out of here?" I whisper into Hex's ear. His hair smells smoky from the cigarette. The ceilingless room is cold and I stay as close to him as I can.

"Don't worry," he tells me. "We have to take turns sleeping. Just don't eat anything, I think it's bewitched. And let me do what I have to."

I don't like the sound of this but I keep watch while he rests his head in my lap and closes his eyes. I think I would be happy to have his weight resting against my crossed legs under other circumstances but I'm too frozen with dread to really feel anything. Even Hex's considerable body heat won't thaw me out.

When Beatrix wakes in the cold, dead dawn, she sends Frakk away and tries to feed us again. She tells Ez to bring us plates of cake. I stare at the porous layers lined with filling and whipped cream and my mouth's salivating like a dog's. Hex, whom I've elbowed awake, politely declines for both of us.

"But I have something to offer you," he says.

She opens her eyes wide as twin hand mirrors. "Oh, yes? Really? What is that?"

"I'll sleep with you," Hex says, smiling that wicked grin with the vampire teeth. "In exchange for our freedom."

She looks like she's going to cry. Her black hair whips around her in a gust of wind, sudden through the ruined walls. Leaves shake and fall to the floor. I'm so cold it's making my shoulder and calf muscles cramp. And I don't want Hex to sleep with her. I put my hand on his arm.

"I have to," he whispers, angling his head back to reach my ear with his mouth. "We're going to die otherwise."

I look at Ez, with frosting in his nostrils; his eyes roll back. Another butterfly is circling him, seemingly unaware of the fate of its crushed friend.

I nod at Hex.

"Why would I agree to that?" Beatrix says through her tears.

"You want me," he says to Beatrix. "Believe me."

I don't know anything anymore about what lies outside myself, only a little about the broken landscape inside. I don't want Hex to go with Beatrix but I can't say anything. I scuttle over as far as my leash reaches and scrounch down next to Ez with frosting all over his face and hair.

Beatrix comes over and touches Hex's face, her fingers lingering. She touches his throat and I can feel mine close up and I gag. She takes his leash and tugs it—almost playfully is how I'd describe it, under other circumstances.

"Remember, don't eat anything." Hex whispers the warning but his eyes are shout-big.

I watch him walk away behind Beatrix. Is she a witch? I think of another Goya painting, this one of a black, horned he-goat surrounded by a gaggle of howling, deformed witches. Beatrix is a pretty witch but she gives my stomach the same queasy, inside-out feeling I'd get looking at those dark works of art.

Then I turn my attention to the cake. All we've had for four days now are canned meats and beans with a tinny aftertaste and stale chips that sting our gums. It's like my mouth is made of salt and dirt. *Don't eat anything.*

I look at Ez instead. "I'm Pen."

He doesn't answer me. His brown eyes seem to have a glaze over them, a sugar cataract. His hands continue to wriggle in his mouth even though the cake is now gone.

"Are you okay? How long have you been here?"

His mouth drops open but he doesn't speak.

"She trapped you here?" My fingers move toward his dog collar but he covers it with his own before I can touch it.

I glance down at the sketch he's made; it's of Beatrix.

The long neck, mystic eyes, and classical features look as Pre-Raphaelite as Beatrix herself. I bet Ez knows who Waterhouse is. Or once did.

"You're a great artist."

He doesn't answer.

"You should come with us," I say. "Hex will handle her."

When I say these words my stomach drops like I'm falling from a great height. I don't want Hex to "handle" Beatrix. I imagine his small hands caught in the sea snakes of her hair. Her fleshy lips, bony-curvy body. She looks like she could crush Hex but he's stronger than he appears.

"Talk to me," I say to Ez. "Tell me your name."

"Do you have any cake?" he asks. "Strawberry pistachio cream cupcakes or anise butter cookies? She gives me plenty. Do you have any sweet buns stuffed with plum lavender jam? Tiger-striped macadamia cinnamon rolls? Fresh peppermint leaf and rose-petal ice cream?"

The frosting in his hair suddenly looks weirdly appetizing to me. As if reading my mind, he pulls a glob out of the strands and eats it. He smiles and his teeth are green from the roses.

"How'd you get here?" I ask.

"I don't know. She found me in a ditch, she says. She bathed and dressed me, gave me my jewelry." He touches his collar. "Then she fed me." His eyes look into the distance, landscapes of whipped cream and layer cake, I imagine. "It is always my birthday here. All I have to do is draw."

"You have to come with us," I say. "You're her prisoner."

He surveys me blankly. "Yes, of course. What else would I want to be?"

"Do you remember before?" I ask. "Do you remember Then?"

"Then does not exist," he says.

"Try to remember. Did you have a family?"

"I had a twin," says Ez. "We were never apart. Then he was gone. Everything was gone."

Two red-haired boys, exactly alike and yet completely different, on a basketball court behind a grand Spanish-style house. One is shooting baskets while the other draws flowers with chalk on the asphalt.

Why am I seeing this image, and so clearly? It's like the vision I had of the child in the pink room. Could this red-haired boy be Ez? Could the other child be Hex? But why am I seeing them this way? It's not like I'm imagining it, but actually *seeing* them.

I reach out with tentative fingers and stroke Ez's red hair, still sticky with frosting. Not Moira-ginger, really red. I expect him to flinch, which he does at first, and then he flutters his eyelids and tilts his head toward me. I continue to pet him like this until . . . finally he closes his eyes and then leans his head on my knee and falls asleep.

In another room Hex is with Beatrix and I tell myself not to visualize his body on top of hers, the swirls of black hair wrapping them both up like toxic waves. I try not to eat frosting out of Ez's hair as he sleeps but suddenly the taste of sugar is what I want. Hex is mine, I think, and then wonder how I could think that. He's never kissed me. I've never even seen him without a shirt on. I know the skin of his chest must be very pale and smooth like the rest of his body; I can see his wide shoulders and his narrow waist.

My brother, Venice, is gone and I'm not dead. But I'm pretty much walking dead, without a heart.

Venice is still my heart, and my heart is missing, but Hex has become my lungs.

When Hex comes out of Beatrix's chamber he looks paler than ever but he doesn't have his collar on. He walks over to me, silent in his rubber-soled basketball shoes.

He's carrying something in his hand—a long sword with a curved steel blade, death-sharp. I recognize it as a traditional Japanese samurai sword or *nihonto*. It has a black handle inlaid with white bone; there's a black iron dragon plate at the hilt.

"Why do you have that?" I ask as he releases me from bondage.

"She gave it to me."

"Do you know how to use it?"

He flashes the sword in the air, swift and graceful as if he's done it a million times before. "I took lessons, once."

I just stare at him, imagining him in a studio with mirrored walls, wearing a samurai costume, his hair bound back from his face, kohl eyes.

"Let's leave," he says. "She says we can leave."

I want to ask him what he did to convince her to let us go, to give him her sword. I want to yell, *What did you do?* I want him to be mine. I want to be able to say, *You are mine, you can't be with anyone else.* But instead I cradle Ez's face in my hands before resting his head on a pillow on the floor.

"We have to bring him," I say. "He's dead otherwise."

"We don't have enough supplies."

"Please, Hex."

He looks down at Ez, then back at me.

"He can have half my food. Please."

"No way. You're too thin already."

Ez opens his eyes and sits up. "We can bring the cake!" he says brightly.

"No cake, yo. You're almost as bad as me with the singing chicks," says Hex, but I can see by the softening of his sword-reflecting eyes that he's going to give in.

As we drag Ez away, all I see, when I look back at the banquet table, are piles of dirt.

10

HOOD CITY

FOR THE NEXT THREE DAYS after this (I've started marking time again, red slashes on the interior of the van), Ez rests in my arms crying for cake while Hex drives. When Hex isn't looking I feed Ez half my portion of canned peaches or black beans, which he sometimes vomits up outside while I hold his forehead. I can see Hex is irritated that Ez is so helpless, another problem for us to handle. But I know when he gets better, Hex will be glad to have one more pair of hands.

I hope.

"Eliot," Ez moans in his sleep the third night.

"Who's Eliot?" I whisper, thinking of my vision—the

basketball-playing boy—and Ez wakes up as if I've shouted it in his ear. We're in the back of the van and Hex is at the wheel.

"What did you say?"

"You were talking in your sleep. You said 'Eliot.' Is that your twin?"

He covers his mouth with his hand. I can almost see the stifled sob in the way his Adam's apple moves.

I speak softly. "I understand. I had a brother. *Have.* I miss him so much."

Ez's expression shifts and his eyes focus as if he's just looked up from staring through a magnifying glass. "I'm so sorry."

"We're going to find him," I say, as if the ferocity of my voice can make it so.

"What is he like?"

"He's perfect. He's ten. He thought he was too short and that his front teeth were too big, that he wasn't good enough at baseball, but he was perfect in every way. And I didn't tell him that. I fought with him sometimes. He was sweet and polite and cared about people. Everyone loved him."

"I think when you have a very close sibling," Ez says, "it makes you feel like you're always supposed to have someone there with you, all the time, someone who understands you. I was always trying to find someone to fall in love with."

"Did you?" I ask.

He gets the blank look in his eyes again. "I'm seventeen and it's never happened. The world's ended and it's never going to happen. I've thought I was in love but they never love me back."

"I understand," I say, thinking of how I once kissed Moira on the lips. We were drunk and dancing and our lips just brushed for that electroshock nanosecond and then she smiled at some boys who were watching us, laughed, and danced away from me like it was a joke. But I'd had an epiphany, even though I hadn't fully accepted it at the time. I wanted to kiss girls. And it was no joke.

"I can be your brother for now. Until we find him."

"And I'll be yours," I say.

I think I can hear Hex letting out a gust of air between his kiss-shaped lips, exasperated with us.

When it's my turn to drive I squint out the window of the VW at the darkness piled with death. I wonder if any love is out there or if what snuggles within the confines of the lime green van is all we will ever know.

Hex sleeps in the back under a rough woolen blanket,

his boots still on. I imagine his long eyelashes stirring with each breath. Moira used to complain about such lashes wasted on boys. Sometime, while Hex sleeps, I want to lean over and feel those eyelashes touch my cheek in a stolen Eskimo kiss.

I am grateful Hex is here with me, that he didn't decide to stay with Beatrix. He could have fallen under her spell like Frakk did, those lilac eyes and veins, her white skin a-glisten, rose petal–like, as if covered with a thin layer of morning dew. But I'm underestimating him, aren't I? He's certainly not Frakk. And he isn't superficial. Though he did say he was a sucker for pretty girls. *It doesn't matter, Pen; he's here.*

Ez is in the passenger seat beside me. I can hear hungry-stomach grumbles but I can't tell if they're his or mine. The supplies that were in the van and the ones I got at the Giant's store are dwindling. We all smell pretty ripe. But perhaps this strange configuration of bodies is love; love is what it is.

In the morning Ez is less weepy and tranced-out as if the spell's been broken. He does a careful inventory of our food and water supply. "Thirty-three cans, twelve boxes of crackers, and forty-two gallons of water. The Red Cross says you need one gallon per person per day. We have enough of everything to last two weeks if we're very careful," he says.

Hex rolls his eyes and Ez adds, "Thank you for bringing me. I know you didn't have to."

I try not to think what happens when the supplies run out. Maybe Hex was right about not bringing Ez but what would have happened to him if we didn't? And if we start living as every man for himself, what does that say about us, the state of our souls?

Still, we have to eat. Although we may eventually find more canned food and bottled water, what about when that's all gone? There are no fresh things growing, no animals to kill and eat, although even as hungry as I am it's hard for me to imagine doing this. Ez probably couldn't either, so I guess it would be up to Hex to hunt.

Ez draws blowsy cabbage roses and candy-striped tulips, as refined as those in a sixteenth-century Dutch or Flemish Renaissance still life, and serves the canned beans on tin plates, setting them before us as if he is giving us a gourmet meal. "Sir, mademoiselle, your food. Beans Baked à la Tin Can from the kitchen of Ezra the gourmand."

I bet he was a great chef. He tells about how to use turmeric to make the rice a golden color and prevent inflammation, how to soak antioxidant-rich goji berries in water to plump them, and add them to quinoa, using chia and hemp seeds for protein.

"As long as you don't mention the junk food," Hex groans. "Because I need to slam some of that shit down now!"

"You could smell the onion rings from a mile away," Ez says. "Toxic waste. I mean grease."

"Now, now," says Hex. "Don't dis my toxic grease. One man's toxic grease is another man's comfort food. And now you've got me talking about it like I said not to!" He chews a knuckle. "Next you're going to bring up cigarettes."

"I'll tell you about spirulina powder," Ez says. "Protein-rich superfood from green algae."

"Blech. That's better."

Since the Earth Shaker, my stomach sometimes hurts like it's being stabbed from inside with little elfin swords. I scrape my spoon over my plate to get the last thin layer of brown sauce, almost lick it but decide not to. Not that Ez or Hex would care, though.

Ez finishes his baked beans and is rummaging around the van looking for hidden cans of extra food, old nutrition bars, anything edible. He finds a compartment built into the back of the van and opens it. "What's this?" he asks. He takes out a large wooden box, painted black. Inside is a map.

Maps always remind me of my brother, how he covered the walls of his room with the free ones we got in the mail and ones he meticulously drew and colored himself. And, something else: Merk mentioned a map. *You need to find them. There's a map in the van.* I'd forgotten.

On this map, a route, marked in yellow neon highlighter, goes from Los Angeles through the desert to Las Vegas.

"This is what he mentioned, right, Pen?" Hex asks, examining it. "He seemed pretty deliberate about giving you the van. I say we go to Vegas."

"I don't think so. Who knows what that guy was doing? It might be some kind of a trap," says Ez.

Hex eyes him sideways. His voice is terse, impatient. "He gave Pen a van with fuel and food. That doesn't sound like a trap to me."

"He said my family might be there," I tell them. "And, anyway, where else will we go?"

But before we follow the route on the map, we decide to go up into the hills to survey the city so we know what we're dealing with if we try to leave. None of us really want to see the truth but this isn't a time for shielding our eyes.

Up what used to be Beachwood Canyon—now a cracked cement road covered with dead palm and cypress trees and lined with fallen Craftsman cottages, Spanish adobes, and Normandy castles in varying states of collapse and ruin. We reach the fire road that leads to the Hollywood sign. It used to read *Hollywoodland* but the letters fell down decades ago; now we've lost the o-l-l-y-w so it just reads *H-O-O-D*.

We park the car behind some rocks, slather ourselves with sunscreen from the Giant's store, and walk on foot. Hood City stretches below us, for as far as we can see—a dark expanse of fallen trees and buildings that look like they were made of carelessly crumpled paper; nothing green; small fires burning, spontaneously, even as we watch. The air stings my eyes and there are particles of soot in my mouth. Here and there, I think I see something big and slow and fleshy lumbering along below us but it could be my imagination.

There is nothing, anywhere, that has not been touched by disaster. I wonder if this is what we'd see if we had an even greater view of the city, the country, the planet.

Ez is standing catatonic, staring out at the view.

"Ez?" I say, afraid; it's like he's back in his cake-induced trance. "You okay?"

He doesn't answer.

"Ez?"

Hex shakes his shoulder. "Snap out of it, man, we don't have time for this."

"I didn't realize it was this bad," Ez says, his eyes blank.

"The Earth Shaker," I say.

"But all the people? Where could they all go?"

"Remember Frakk?" I say. "There are more like him."

"I thought I hallucinated that. I mean, Giants with pig heads?"

"Unfortunately you didn't," says Hex. "Times are hard on the boulevard. I saw that written on a wall once."

Ez puts his hands over his face and starts to cry, little breathy gasps, his shoulders shaking.

I put my arms around him. We're both so thin that our collarbones bump, hard. "It's going to be okay."

"No, it's not! My family's all dead. My brother . . ."

I try to make soothing sounds but I'm thinking of my own family—what they thought of when they saw the wave coming, terror like being held in a Giant's palm—and it's hard to be of comfort. "Do you want to talk about it?"

"No!" Ez looks at me like I've slapped him. "I don't want to talk. I want to die. Life was hard enough before."

Hex breaks a twig with his boot. "Be glad you're not dead. We're the lucky ones."

"Lucky?" Ez glares at him through a film of tears. "How are we lucky?"

"You had a family," he snarls. "Not everyone does. And you lost them but you're alive. You have a chance. They don't."

"Listen, stop!" I sound like my mom breaking up an argument between Venice and my younger self. "Stop it! Let's get out of here."

There's one more place I want to see before we leave this town.

11

THE MUSEUM
OF ANGELS

A S WE DRIVE THERE I explain to my friends—
there are three reasons I want to go to the
museum.

One, my mom took us almost every weekend since
before I could walk. We did arts and crafts in the courtyard, explored one gallery each time, and ate croissant
sandwiches at the café.

Two, some of my favorite works of art are there—
Monet's *Nymphéas* with the large water lilies, a melding,
glowing blur of color and light, painted by an artist losing
his sight to cataracts. Georges de la Tour's *Magdalen*, which
seems like there's a candle burning behind the canvas.

Rodin's bronzes—the centauress, her human torso strain-
ing to be free of her animal haunches, the devilish mino-
taur grappling with a naked nymph, the crouching woman
who looks like she's either giving birth to the earth or
being born from it. Robert Graham's column has doll-
sized, bald, naked women half-emerging from inside (or
imprisoned, it's hard to tell).

Three (and this is also a reason I *don't* want to go): to
see if any of it still remains. In spite of the impressive
exterior with clustered old-fashioned street lamps and
modern black stone waterfalls, the Los Angeles County
Museum always seemed a little apocalyptic to me because
of the tar pits.

We arrive at what was once a park and see black goo
gubbling up from the ground; in ancient times it claimed
mastodons and preserved their bones for scientists to
study. I wonder what will happen now—who, if anyone,
will find our remains and trace them back to a civilization that self-destructed. I'm afraid to think about what
has happened to the works of art inside the buildings
but from what I can see in the near distance, the struc-
tures are still standing and this makes me curious.

"We should leave," Hex says as we stand at the edge of
the tar pits, gazing up at the museum buildings to the
west. There used to be a father-and-baby mastodon statue

on the shore, watching the mother drown in the tar, but now all three statues lie broken, belly up in the black pool. "I have a bad feeling. I've seen enough."

Ez nods in agreement.

"Please," I say, tugging on Hex's T-shirt sleeve. The collar pulls away from his tattooed neck and his tendons look taut as the strings of a musical instrument. "Just really quickly. I want to see inside, if anything is left."

He frowns at me. "I need a cigarette."

"Please, Hex." I look at Ez, thinking of his masterful sketches of Beatrix and the Dutch still-life sketches on napkins. "What if the art is still there? We need some art. You're like me, right, Ez? You need it. Like food."

"He needs his jugular more." Hex puts his fingers lightly around Ez's throat and Ez acquiesces. Poor Ez; he's at Hex's mercy. "Those monsters could be there." At first I think he's still joking when he says this but there's something different in his voice, under the tease. Fear? I want to be the one in charge this time. Convince him that I can be brave, too. Protect him if I have to. But I don't think I will have to.

"What are you going to do if you find art, Pen? You going to steal some and put it in the van?"

"I'm going to remember," I say. "When there was

art." The images are stories. They help me to escape.
They help me to see.

Ez nods. "I want to remember that, too. There was a
Hindu watercolor of eight mother goddesses on animals
fighting these little white, bloody demons."

"There are lots of demons," Hex says, eyeing the smoky
skyline. "Do you really need to go into a museum to see
them?"

But he goes with us anyway.

We enter the oldest building first. The glass door has
been smashed but inside the dark rooms the art still
hangs on the walls. We walk around warily; Hex has his
sword drawn. I can't believe how much is still here. Why
hasn't it been destroyed or looted? A shiver like chipped
ice slides down my spine.

On the wall before me, lit by a thin beam from the
skylight, is a drawing by Odilon Redon of a hot air bal-
loon shaped like a blown-up human eye. I saw a print in
my mother's art book of a Redon painting of a hillside,
that looks made of petals, insect wings, and semiprecious
stones, on which lies a sleeping nude woman. A bald
Cyclops with protruding ears hovers above her. It used
to register as almost charming to me, the shy-seeming

monster. Now the thought of the single floating blue eye makes me sicken and cringe.

I turn to an oil painting by Elihu Vedder of a landscape of clouds above peeling-back layers of dark teal, jade, and white surf. It's called *Memory* and if you look closely you can see a child's face emerging from the sky. It reminds me of Venice, the way his sweet, round face floats in the clouds of my mind. I turn to call my friends over, to show them . . .

Then the building shakes.

"Pen!" I hear Hex calling for me but I can't see him. The room is too dark and now the wall in front of me is cracking into pieces, the art falling to the floor, glass frames shattering.

Something is here with us.

Something grunting, reaching out a massive hand to me.

"My bride," he says.

12

THE GIANT'S BRIDE

AS THE BUILDING CRUMBLES around me, crumbles to dust, I am lifted up and carried away in that hand. I'm screaming for Hex and it feels like an organ is being torn slowly out of my unanesthetized body. Hex and Ez are there, in that building. I'm pleading and screaming and kicking. The thing lifts me out into the gray light of day. Stink of tar in the air. I see his face; he looks like the Giant I blinded but he has two looming eyes.

"Please!" I say. "My friends are there! Please!"

"No friends. You are my bride. I must fatten you."

"My friends! Please don't leave them there." In

delirium I'm asking for him to go after them? But better than seeing them crushed to death—somehow we could escape a Giant more easily than an earthquake? Or is it better? Could we escape, even together?

"No," he says again.

He carries me to the other museum building, the newer one with the high ceilings. He grabs the flimsy partitions, cracks them between his hands, and thrusts them aside, leaving space so he can walk through the rooms.

A delicate bed with a pale blue hand-painted headboard, decorated with clouds, ribbons, and cherubs, stands waiting. He places me on it, holding me with his thumb—the thick, clammy weight on my chest—while he uses rope to fasten me there. Bristling, braided rope cutting into my skin.

"I must fatten you."

He exits, heavy footsteps making the room shake, but it doesn't fall. I wish it would. I scream for Hex and Ez until my throat is raw as if with infection. The room spins and grows dimmer and then goes black.

When I wake it's to the smell of food. Steaming, fatty meat, the first meat I've seen in months. It's glistening on a plate in front of me. The Giant is crouched down watching my face.

"You must eat."

Meat. But there are no animals to hunt. Only a few humans . . .

I feel whatever small amount of food is in my belly gurgling up. I cover my mouth with my hand and shake my head.

"My bride must be fat."

I shake my head, gritting my teeth to hold back vomit. No.

"You will stay with me and give me sons."

A terror as of something ripping my body in half. I turn my head away, flailing under the rope trying to free myself, chafe burns at my wrists and ankles. "Let me go!"

The meat. What is it? Who is it? I scream for my friends as if they can hear me. I think, *I will be slaughtered and eaten. Like this.*

I have no scissors, no sword, even my voice is failing me, turning into a wretched squeak. I stare at the meat. The Giant tears off and holds up a long strip. Then he pinches at my jaws the way you would do to a stubborn dog and tries to shove the meat into my mouth. I bite at his hand and he slaps me so my head snaps back.

When my jaw falls open he wrestles the meat in and

covers my mouth with his palm until I swallow it down. The gaminess. I can taste nerve endings. My eyes fill up with tears. He does it again. Strip, pinch, shove, slap. And again. Then he leaves.

All I want is to stick my fingers down my throat as far as they will go but I can't move my bound hands.

But my merciful body takes over, spewing the unchewed meat across the floor.

I lie in the darkness with something boiling inside of me like I'm going to explode. What I keep seeing, again and again, is a giant Beatrix ballooned to ten times her normal size, lying on an ornate bed with Hex pinned to her naked breast like a broach.

Delirium. What is nightmare, what is hallucination? What is reality? There was a night when my parents were fighting:

"They're doing something. Evil. I can't tell you. They could harm us. Maybe I should go away," my dad said.

"David, you're not making sense. What do you mean by evil?" My mom wept.

My pillowcase was wet with tears and mucus. At least Venice was at a sleepover, not having to hear. If he were there I would have run to him, held him, comforting myself just as much that way. But it was better he wasn't there. Was our father going crazy? Would we lose our home, have to live on the streets? Noey didn't have room for us; Moira's mom would never take us in. Fear is a Giant. It feels like something was pushing at me, breaking me open, turning me inside out. My mother was crying. She didn't come to me because she couldn't hear me through her sobs. Is that why? She didn't come.

But then I hear. I hear the voices, soft as the wind in non-existent trees. "Pen, hold on."

"Hex?"

Like a vision, like a Pre-Raphaelite painting of an androgynous-looking hero come to life. He has his sword at his side and with it he slices the ropes and sets me free. I'm trembling and nauseated, shaking when I stand, but I lean against him and Ez and they lead me out of there, my rescuers, alive. I have no idea how long it's been. . . .

The van waits for us by the tar pit. The Giant is nowhere to be seen.

"I'm so sorry," I say, sobbing, curled in the backseat with Ez as Hex drives. "I thought you were dead. I thought . . ."

"Hush now, sparkle princess. Hush. We've got you."

"He said he wanted me to make him sons. He fed me something . . ." I'm going to vomit again. "What did I eat?"

Ez holds my head on his lap. "You're safe, okay. You're safe. Everything is going to be okay."

"No more stops," Hex says. "Even for art's sake, baby. We're blowing this nasty town."

When I wake up I'm screaming for water. "I ate it! I threw up but I ate it. What did I eat?"

Ez is driving and Hex lifts me to a seated position and holds me against his chest while I sip the water he gives me. "It's over now."

"But what was it? That I ate. Was it human?"

"The Giants probably have animal meat," Ez says. "I'm sure it was an animal."

"Pen." Hex makes me look at him. "It's over. We don't have the time or energy to look back now. Okay? We're all safe."

My hands go to my head. There is something in my hair, drying, crusting now. I recoil. "What's in my hair!" I pull-pull-pull at it, screaming.

Hex grabs my wrists and holds me still.

"Cut it off! Shave it off. I don't want hair. I don't want to be . . . I don't want a body. It's not safe! Cut off my hair."

"Pen?"

"Now! Hex, now! You understand! I know you understand. Now!"

"When we stop the van," he promises, as if speaking to a child. "When we stop, I'll cut it. We have to keep going now. To get away."

Hex holds me close for the next hour or so, calling me baby girl, singing me snatches of songs. Later, he does as he promised, carefully trimming my hair close to the scalp, then using precious water and soap to wet and lather and shave away the hairs that are left. I'm clean. I'm like a boy. Don't even need to see my reflection. It doesn't matter how I look. I can breathe again. I can speak.

"How did you survive? The building looks like it collapsed." I try to keep myself from crying but tears tickle and prick in the corners of my eyes, so strongly I feel the sensation in my naked scalp.

"Ez did something. I don't know what." Hex reaches into the front seat and grasps Ez's shoulder, in a way he's never done before. A solid touch, a touch of equals. "I don't know if I thanked you, homey."

In the rearview mirror I see Ez's smile spreading. "You just did."

I rub my eyes when he and Hex bump fists; did I really just see that? It's not Hex's usual style. "What happened? Ez?"

"I grabbed him when I saw the wall falling and I prayed really hard?"

"But it was more than that," says Hex. "The part of the building where we were just sort of separated from the rest of it after he lifted you out of there. It was like some kind of magic shit."

I remember holding up my hand to the wave when the Earth Shaker hit. Did I stop that wave? Did I save myself? Was there magic at work then?

Some kind of wickedy magic that has preserved us in this hell, without our loved ones. But we have one another and Hex, our intrepid leader, has told me not to look back.

13

ASH

THE GIANT CABAZON T-REX and Apatosaurus are a roadside attraction on the way to the desert, and I can't believe they're still standing after practically everything else has been flattened. But stand they do, perfect symbols of our extinct, monstrously swollen world, and the right size for the Giants who inhabit it. Even so, we're a ways out of L.A., there aren't any Giants visible around here, and there isn't much place for them to hide, so Hex thinks it's safe to go scavenging for food. We park and sunscreen up and walk under a large sign that cruelly reads: "EAT." (Cruel in two ways—because we're hungry and we don't want to be any beast's dinner.)

While Hex stands guard with his sword, Ez and I explore the gift store inside the three-story T-Rex. Maybe there will be some candy or soda. I don't hesitate because I saw an orange butterfly flash by me at the entrance.

We hear singing, ethereal, as if from a cathedral. Ez spots the young man first, wandering in a daze down the empty aisles. He has dark skin and the face (and voice) of a Byzantine angel and he says his name is Ash.

"There used to be food," he muses, full lips parting to reveal small, perfect teeth. "Have you seen any food lately?"

Ez says gently, as if trying not to make him bolt at the news, "I don't think there's much food here anymore."

"Oh, yeah, I guess," says Ash. "Do you think we can get some macaroni and cheese? I really like that."

"I know." Ez speaks just to him. "Food is good." His voice sounds wistful and dreamy, the way it sounded when he spoke about cake a week ago. I wonder if I should step away and let them talk privately.

Ash is staring at Ez with his long, green eyes in a way that makes me uncomfortable, as if I've walked in on something.

"There's no more food?" Ash asks. His bottom lip pouts but I think that's just how it's formed.

"Are you alone?" Ez asks him. "Are you with anyone?"

Ash shakes his head no. "I was on a photo shoot here when it happened."

I notice a few small silk tassels hiding in the mass of his dusty-looking brown dreadlocks. His body is delicate, long and awkward in the expensively shrunken but filthy green sharkskin suit he wears. I used to wonder at the awkwardness of the best models in Moira's magazines and online, their ungainly legs and arms, their oddly shaped noses, wide-spaced eyes, and long necks. Moira could have modeled; we always told her that. Noey said I could have, too, but I would never have wanted to; I preferred to be invisible. It's hard to think of a world where there was a profession involving attractive people dressing up in expensive clothes to have their pictures taken.

"You should come with us," Ez says. "We have a van. We have some food."

I try to catch his eye; what the hell is he doing? We don't have food to share. Hex will kill him. I can see him through the window, pacing around in the dust with his sword, shoulders tight with worry. I want to knead them with my fingers.

How can we take Ash? We need to get moving. I've already waited too long to get to Las Vegas. It might even be too late, if my family was ever there at all. But how can we leave Ash here all alone? I remember Ez crying in my arms.

I was always trying to find someone to fall in love with. . . . It's never happened. The world's ended, and it's never going to happen.

If the world has ended, what else do we have but these last feeble dreams? Plus, Ash is tall and looks strong in spite of his willowiness, and I think we could use another member in our tribe. Another pair of eyes and hands—he could drive the van and we'd have more time to rest and gather our strength. And Ash can sing. Hex hasn't yet heard that voice.

Ash won't take his eyes off of Ez, who looks over at me, and it really is like a light went on inside of him. The dull, glazed look is entirely burned through, gone. "Is it okay if Ash comes, Pen? Oh, this is Pen. I'm Ezra. Ez."

Ash doesn't even glance at me; he's still staring at Ez, the three of us in the belly of a T-Rex in the middle of nowhere. He's the one in a daze now.

"It's funny how you meet people," Ash says.

14

LOVE IN THE TIME OF GLOBAL WARMING

HEX IS ANGRY, OF COURSE. "What the hell, homes?"

I like it better when he calls me sparkle princess. But I get why he's mad. Another stabbingly hungry belly, another fearful psyche to drive around.

He and I are standing by the van while Ez and Ash talk, heads close together, under the shadow of the dinosaurs.

"Ez needs him," I say. "Look at them."

"Ez *needs* him? Ez needs food, and water. And so do we."

"But we have . . ." I was going to say *each other*. As

important as food and water but I can't acknowledge that to him yet. "There was an orange butterfly."

"A what?" The tendons strain in his neck, under the tattoo.

"When I met you. And Ez. And now Ash. Orange butterflies. They keep appearing." I haven't mentioned them before, afraid he'd think I was crazy. Maybe I am. "Forget it."

I turn away from him but he grabs my wrist and pulls me back.

A flash of heat passes between us, like something wet dropped in a scalding pan.

"I remember that one at the hotel. And when we met Ez. You think they're some kind of sign?"

Yes. "My mom loved them. She had butterfly tattoos and made collages with butterfly wings. I know I sound insane."

Ash and Ez approach us and Hex kicks at the dirt; dust rises up, making me cough.

Ash takes a canteen out of his pocket and hands it to me. "Water?" he says. "I found a supply in the casino but it's almost out."

I thank him and tell him we have our own. He insists and the dust is hurting my throat so I take one small sip.

There's a boy playing piano. The piano takes up the whole room. The boy's eyes are closed. He plays faster and louder, as if to drown out the sound of glass breaking in the kitchen. Tears run down his face and into his mouth but he doesn't wipe them away.

This is Ash, I realize, Ash as a child. Another vision, like what I saw of Hex and Ez. With each one it's as if I'm finding some missing puzzle piece. Or just another confirmation of the madness that is overtaking me. But what is madness in such a world? My eyes meet Hex's. *Please.*

"I know where there is more water, I think," Ash says. "I can smell it on the wind." He closes his eyes and breathes in like a noble dog leaning its head out the window of a moving car (*Argos, I remember you, I have not forgotten*), and points into the distance. "If there was fresh water anywhere it would be there. The Oasis in Twenty-nine Palms. But I don't have a car."

Please, Hex. Ez's wish is so loud I can almost hear it.

"I know that place," Hex says. He turns to me. "He may be right. And it's on the way."

To confirm, an orange butterfly appears, as if an

invisible magician snapped his fingers in the air, and lands on Ash's dreadlocks like a colorful barrette. Hex catches my eye, throws the key to Ash. "We're wiped. You can drive, dude."

Ez grabs my hand and squeezes. He thanks Hex, who shrugs.

"I owed you—whatever magic you did back there in the museum. . . . Now we're even."

Without thinking about it, I lean over and kiss his cheek. It's so soft and smooth, like a child's.

"Come on," he says, not looking at me, turning, flinging up his hands. "What are you all waiting for? The end of the world?"

We've spent the last day driving and talking. Mostly we talked about food, music, art, books, the things we miss about Then. Sometimes Hex read to us from *The Odyssey*, although it frightens me after all the parallels. We avoided talk of the Earth Shaker as we drove through the pass where the windmills used to be. Most of them are broken now, and lie in heaps as if a huge child had become infuriated with his toys.

We were trying to distract ourselves from the danger of being this out in the open. The road through the desert wasn't really any less safe than the city roads, but the lack of rubble (only some fallen billboards and deserted shells of cars) made us feel more vulnerable.

"I grew up on junk food," Hex admitted after we had left an old fast food place, ransacked except for the rancid vegetable oil cans that we took for fuel. (Hex stuck his sword into the ground and raised his hands with triumph when we found the oil and I whispered, "Maybe this guy is good luck," meaning Ash. Hex said, "I wouldn't go that far.")

"The worst crap," Hex said. "Cheeseburgers, fries, whatever, garbage. Sometimes I dream I'm holding this giant cheeseburger with the pink sauce stuff spilling out the side and I wake up crying. I swear I can smell the grease."

"My parents never let us eat junk food," I said. Then I asked, "What about yours?" I realized we'd never talked about them before.

He laughed but it sounded more like a cough, dusty and dry in his throat. "They were gone most of the time. At work, at parties. I was alone in this big house with a load of cash and a fake ID. So I bought whiskey and drugs and junk food. It was awesome. Good times." His eyes went hard when he said it.

"My mom didn't care either," said Ash, unconsciously pulling at a dreadlock with elongated fingers. "She was at work so I made frozen pizza or cold cereal for dinner every night. When I started working I spent all my money at restaurants."

Ez said he liked raw and vegan. "Millet, mung beans, coconut oil, flax seeds, acai berries."

We passed another mountainous stack of cleanly gnawed bones but none of us commented on it. Maybe it was perverse to talk food but somehow it made the carnage seem less real.

"Did you ever try those raw desserts?" Ez asked, almost defiantly, I thought, in the face of the bones. "The cashew ice cream? It was insane. I made it, too. It was even better. Coconut milk, dates . . ."

"Stop, I'm getting hungry," I said. "Pen thinks it sounds blissiant," Hex teased, and I punched him. Not hard.

"Raw cacao truffles?" Ez went on. "Ever try one?"

"If you could have any meal you want for dinner tonight, what would it be?" Ash asked.

"I'd like to say quinoa . . ."

"What? How do you even spell that?"

"It's a supergrain, Hex. Let me finish. Kale cooked in coconut oil, butternut squash soup, brown rice avocado sushi rolls." Ez paused. "But really? Chocolate layer cake, vanilla cake with strawberry whipped cream filling, mocha fudge swirl. Cake for days. No healthy raw desserts for me right now. Not if we're fantasizing. Lemon meringue cake."

I wasn't surprised about the cake, remembering Beatrix. That witch knew his weaknesses. Luckily, Hex knew hers was sexy young men. I still don't know what happened between them but I can guess and sometimes it makes my heart beat so fast that I can't breathe.

"Pie," Hex corrected Ez. "It was lemon meringue pie."

"No, it was cake, too. I had it once from a bakery called Angel something. The filling was like clouds. It was serious insanity."

"I'd want a cheeseburger and fries and a chocolate cookie milkshake," Hex said. "And a diet soda."

"Diet soda?" I squeaked. "That's the worst thing for you. And why diet? Look at you!" I pinched his ribs and he batted my hand away, grinning. "It tastes like chemicals and rotten fish."

"What? You're concerned about my *imaginary* diet soda? Really? I guess you won't let me have any imaginary cigarettes either?"

I stuck my tongue out at him and he winked at me.

"It's better than the shit I used to put in my body, believe me."

"I'd even settle for frozen pizza and cold cereal at this point," Ash said.

"What about you, Pen?"

I thought of my mom's dinners, each dish infused

with love. There was a shiitake mushroom spinach quiche she made, with a buttery crust, a lentil soup served with homemade corn bread, tomato-ey ratatouille with pine nuts, smoked baba ghanoush, wild salmon croquettes with honey wasabi dipping sauce. My stomach hurt—fiercely—and I shook my head.

Later, Hex read aloud to us:

"*But leave me now to eat my dinner, for all my sorrow, for there is no other thing so shameless as to be set over the belly, but she rather uses constraint and makes me think of her, even when sadly worn, when in my heart I have sorrow as now I have sorrow in my heart, yet still forever she tells me to eat and drink and forces me to forgetfulness of all I have suffered, and still she is urgent that I must fill her.*'"

"No more belly talk, please," I begged, even though what I really meant was home talk.

So Hex brought up music. "It was invented so man could speak to God," he said.

"Do you believe in God?" Ash asked. It was the first time any one of us had mentioned the subject.

Hex paused, only briefly. "I believe in music. It's in our genetics. There's even a gene for it. Like songbirds have."

And, like songbirds, we spent the rest of the day singing, for one another, our favorite tunes. Hex knows the lyrics to them all. They sound exotic, magical and strange, these popular songs about love, where all that was at stake was your heart.

Ash's voice is mellifluous; when we asked what his favorite music was, he said, "I like the *Four Seasons* by Vivaldi." Hex and Ez looked at him, surprised. Not me, so much; I'd had that vision of him playing the piano. . . .

"*What?*" he said, defensive.

"You just don't seem like the classical type," said Hex. "I would have guessed indie, art, emo."

Ash shrugged and tapped long brown fingers on the dashboard. "Do you think we'll ever hear a concerto again?"

As if in answer something went dark—the sun had suddenly set or a rain cloud had moved in?—but when we looked, we saw it was a hulking figure looming on the horizon, still as stone, eyes closed as if asleep.

Now we're parked behind an outcropping of rock. Usually we keep going, one person at the wheel while the others sleep, but sometimes we need to just stop for a while and feel the ground motionless under us as we rest.

I want to get out of the stuffy, sweaty van and smell the sand and desert air but I remember how we can't risk being without the little protection we have in case anything comes, in case the Giant on the now-distant hill wakes. Also, when it's as cold as this your fingers feel like they're so swollen and burning with pain that they'll fall off if you rub them together to warm them. As if he's heard my thoughts, Hex takes my hands and holds them in his lap so I can feel the thick denim of his jeans.

"Are you okay?"

"Yeah. You?"

"You're not okay," he says.

I want him to kiss me. I want to tell him that sometimes I imagine him and Beatrix together in a bed made of branches. I'm grateful to him for freeing us but I don't like the idea of him at the mercy of Beatrix's lips with their pornographic swell, the dark intoxstasy of her hair.

I glance back at Ez and Ash asleep in each other's arms, Ez's head tucked under Ash's chin.

"Thank you for letting Ash come," I say.

"I don't like that twee suit he wears."

"He was modeling it. And there aren't exactly a lot of clothing options anymore."

Hex winks, so fast I'm not sure I saw it. "But it wasn't up to me, anyway. Outvoted."

"Yes, but you are the strongest of us, Prince Charming."

"What did you just call me?"

"If you can call me sparkle princess—I just mean, you could have made the final call."

He shrugs. "You're stronger than you know. And there were those butterflies, after all."

Without looking at him I smile, grateful he understands. "Ez was wrong about love," I say. "Miracles of love still do occur, I guess."

Hex nods. His voice is serious now, almost grave. "Of course, Pen. Had you given up?"

I look out at some shrubs shaking in the wind. "I've given up on everything."

"Even me?"

"Sometimes I think about what happened with Beatrix."

"You're jealous?" Hex is smiling and I can see the flash of his vampiric incisors. The tip of his nose is perfectly sculpted with a little flare of bone above either nostril.

"Not jealous, I just . . ."

"It was battle," he says. "Strategy, nothing else." He

slumps in the seat and runs his hands down the length of his thighs.

"Okay."

"I did what I had to do. It was dark." He pauses, patting his pockets like he's trying to find a cigarette. "Pen, I'm not exactly the person you think I am."

"What does that mean?" I've had enough surprises. I want everything to remain as much the same as possible within the confines of this van, where we've finally established some safety.

"I've been with a lot of people, since I was really young."

"Okay," I say. "I kind of figured that out. Pretty girls and everything . . ."

Wind rocks the van and I tense, thinking, at first, it's a hand.

"I can't really count how many. I couldn't do the whole monogamy thing very well."

Now the tension isn't about being in a Giant's clutches. At least not an actual Giant's. "Okay," I say again—third time—shifting in the seat.

"But I want to, now."

I can't look at him; I can tell our gaze might light something on fire.

"And I wasn't always a boy," he adds. "My name was Alexandria. I called myself Lex at first."

Non sum qualis eram. I am not what I once was. Written boldly on his body.

I'm more shocked by the first statement than the second. He wants to be monogamous? *With me?* He wasn't always male. *So what?* The vision I had of him in the pink room was my first clue. And it's been on his skin anyway, clearly there the whole time. *Non sum qualis eram. I am not what I once was.*

I think of Moira. How I used to feel such wonder at the way her cells had joined together to form the miracle of her. Now this love was just another loss in a sea bubbling with corpses of loss. My crush had ceased to matter because everything had ended and it seemed trivial now to have ever worried about my sexual identity, especially in a family that was so open-minded. But then there were still the politicians and the preachers screaming about family values and hell and it had made me doubt myself, even though I knew better. I'd stopped worrying about it all in the midst of so much real loss and grief. I had forgotten what I thought about sexuality, except that I liked to be near Hex, that I liked to hear his voice, to watch him hunkered down, staring out at the ruined horizon, black steel-toed motorcycle boots kicking at the dirt like he was trying to find something buried there. His gender seemed irrelevant. All I knew

was that I didn't want him to touch anyone else, even as a
strategy.

Hex pulls at the neck of his T-shirt like he's too hot,
like the collar is too constricting for that slender neck
with its Latin words. Then he hesitates, looks at me, deep,
and pulls the shirt over his head. His ribs stick out and
his chest is slight and very white beneath a large tattoo
of an anatomically correct human heart and the word
Heartless.

"That's one thing you're not," I say.

"I'm not what I once was."

"I don't give a fuck what you are or were. I just don't
want you to go away. Ever." Tears squeeze out of my desert-
dry eyes, streaking the dust on my face.

Hex leans over and runs his hands over the prick-
ling stubble that has grown in on my scalp. Part of me
wishes I had hair again, long hair, like Then, wishes I
had Beatrix-hair, pretty-girl-hair to let him lose himself
in. But it doesn't matter. I can feel his mouth kissing
my face, his tongue licking at my tears. *Her.* It doesn't
matter.

"I love you, Pen," Hex says. "You are the who I love."

As my lips become indistinguishable from Hex's, it
is like the stirring of a hundred orange butterfly wings
around us, fanning to life a perfect flame. I can see the

fire tearing over the planet, not a force of destruction but of renewal, a prescribed fire like farmers sometimes used, wiping out all the debris and waste and death so that something new can grow.

The world might be gone but somehow, here with Hex, it feels like when we open our eyes it will all come back, so much better than before.

15

OASIS OF TARA

AROUND US STRETCHES MORE DESERT, harsh and blank except for rocks. Even the Joshua trees are gone, all of them, as if violently harvested, ripped from the ground by huge, rough hands. The Cahuilla Native Americans used to eat the white flowers and the seeds of the Joshua trees' pale green fruit. My mouth salivates to think of this. When my family and I drove to Joshua Tree for a camping trip years ago, I never thought I'd want to get down on my knees and weep for the lost plants, never thought that, in spite of the warnings, they'd ever really become extinct.

None of us speak. In the backseat, Ez rests his head

on Ash's shoulder. Hex doesn't even hum one of his songs from Then like he usually does. He's probably sung half the hip-hop and emo/alternative hits from the last five years over the last week.

We've driven for two days to get here, making our way around junk and cracks in the road, using up most of Merk's fuel and some of the extra rancid vegetable oil from the fast food place. We kept driving anyway, taking turns at the wheel. Although the landscape has been rather merciless, it is, in some ways, easier to take than the ruined city with all its reminders of what once was. Most important, it's on the way to Las Vegas and Ash thinks we'll find water soon. But now I'm starting to doubt our decision.

I am biting my nails so that the tips of my fingers are peeling and raw. We really shouldn't have come out this way, I think. What if Merk and his map was all BS? Are we on a suicide mission and just too cowardly to admit it to ourselves? Are we all already dead? That would make the most sense of all.

But when the sun is highest in the sky, beating down on us without the protective layer of ash that blankets the city, Hex points out the window to forms in the distance. The sunlight blinds me and the world goes white.

"It's a mirage," Ez says. "It has to be."

The light does tremble, miragelike, but as we go closer we all see tall fan palms clustered together and I swear I can smell water. I want to run to the majestic scaly-trunked trees, dripping with fronds and green light and put my arms around them but Hex says no and fastens his sword to his waist.

"We have to check this out first."

We park the van and get out, then walk through a gate. There's a swimming pool, empty save for a small amount of muddy residue. The building beside it has broken windows. We walk in slowly, Hex in front with the sword drawn instead of hanging from his waist where he usually wears it when we explore.

"Anybody here?" Hex shouts.

Inside are empty booths, a sticky bar covered with sharded glass. There's a sweetish-rotten smell under the smell of spilled alcohol and we don't want to know what it is so we leave quickly and walk out the gate again, toward the palm trees.

They grow thickly, reflected in a lake of dark green water that smells like minerals, like life, not like death. I want to hold on to the trees until I turn into one, like a nymph in a mythological tale. There are more plants, too. Silver-green willow and cottonwood and arrowweed with lavender flowers. I can hear, or imagine I hear—a sound like . . . birds? Could it be? A small red houseboat floats on the center of the lake.

The girl—she must be about sixteen—is seated cross-legged on the shore, under a spiky, red-flowering crown of thorns bush. Her hair is piled loosely on her head, some strands falling down over her shoulders. She's draped in thin ruby-red cloth and I can see her breasts through the fabric. The only thing more mesmerizing is her face, which is round with kind lips and high cheekbones. Her skin is sunlit satin. I would guess she is only a teenager but as I get closer I see that her dark, slanted eyes look somehow very old and wise. In one hand she holds a glass vial from which she is dropping liquid onto the ground and as the light of the setting sun catches the glass, red sparks shoot into my face. There is a flock of orange butterflies around her, the most I've ever seen together in one place except for the time my parents took me and Venice to a butterfly tent at the Natural History Museum.

The girl looks familiar but I can't figure out why until Hex whispers, "The mural at the Lotus Hotel."

Yes, that was her, on the wall. Even the petals swarming around her like insects, even the necklaces at her throat like crystal bones and the bangles on her wrists like snakes made of metal. Someone saw her and drew her on the wall, unable to accept that she was "gone."

Wasn't that what art was, after all? Desperate artists telling stories, drawing images, in order to keep some part of the goddess alive and close?

When she tells us her name, it becomes even clearer. Tara.

Tara? Maybe she truly is the Tibetan goddess. Wait. What am I thinking?

Hex lowers his sword and bows his head. I kneel before her and bury my face in my hands to hide the tears. I don't know why I'm crying just now. But I can't stop. Hex puts his hand on my back and more tears release with the pressure of his fingertips.

I've missed you, Tara, I think, which doesn't make any sense. *I longed for you.* It's as if I'm speaking to a part of myself that was severed from me.

"Why have you come?" she asks, her mouth perpetually curved as if smiling, but not quite, her voice tinkling wind chimes. "How did you get here?"

It's Hex who speaks. "We have a van."

She closes her eyes. Her eyelids shimmer, swaths of sunlight in the shade of the palm trees. "You are looking for someone?" And I know that we were meant to come here.

"My family," I whisper, the words scraping my throat like sandpaper.

Tara's eyes open and she looks around her, past the green enclave of the oasis, toward the empty white sky. I am aware of a stirring in the palms that makes me uneasy.

She stands in silence, fingertips to lips, and beckons for us to follow her; she has a very light, dancing step. She's swaying her hips. I don't worry that Hex is falling in love with her because I have already fallen in love with her, too. But not in the way I love him. Hex, I want to kiss all the time like we did in the van last night; for some reason that I don't quite understand I want to worship at the young woman's feet with the delicate metatarsal bones and the small silver rings on the toes. The butterflies still surround her, forming an animated cloak.

We cross a creaking, slatted bridge to the houseboat. Inside it is dark, with a low ceiling, and smells of dried grasses and flowers. Glass jars of dried herbs and pickled foods line the wooden shelves, also small bottles of colored tinctures that our hostess says can purify questionable water or add nutrients to the soil and canned food. There's a small U-shaped wooden harp, a bed draped in diaphanous cloth, and cushions on the floor. Most of the butterflies have stayed outside but a few of the more tenacious ones decorate her hair and collarbone.

It's cramped with all of us here. Ash has to bend his

head to fit, though the rest of us aren't that tall. We sit awkwardly on the floor and Tara brews us tea over a small fire pit. The tea smells rich and medicinal and when I sip it there is the taste of twigs. A slight coating covers my mouth as if I've been licking a plant with furry leaves.

Ash asks if he can see the harp, which he calls a lyre. I'm surprised that he knows the real name. He holds it in his lap like an infant, but doesn't play.

Tara sits cross-legged on the floor and tells us that her parents owned the inn but she's the only one left. She was in the mountains gathering herbs when the Earth Shaker hit and somehow she and her oasis were spared. Like us. After it happened she began to have visions. "Everyone was taken from me but in exchange I received this sight." Her voice is somnambulant and I wonder about her sanity, but then, who am I to wonder that?

"I see the lost living," she says. "I saw you three before you came. I see a woman. But she's almost gone. I think there is also a boy."

I grab Hex's hand without even realizing I'm doing it. "Where?" I say but my mouth is so parched the words are like slivers of dry skin.

So Hex says it louder for me. "Where?"

"You have to start in the Afterworld," she says. "I'm sorry."

Afterworld? I don't like the sound of that.

"Are they both there?" Hex asks.

She shakes her head. "Only the mother. And she is a prisoner of your greatest enemy. He discovered that she is your mother. It will take great sacrifice but that is your only chance."

"How do we get there?" I ask, trying to keep my voice from rising in pitch to the pure desperation I feel. "Where is Venice? My brother?"

"You have to go to the place called Sin," she says as she sips her tea. "The place that had all the lights. The mother is there."

So it's not as bad as I thought. It's a place where the living can go.

"Las Vegas?" Hex asks.

Ez frowns and leans closer to him. "How does she know?" He looks at Tara. "No disrespect, but why should we trust you?"

"It's on the map," I say, thinking of the yellow lines, shining neon. As if this explains her clairvoyance. Or maybe it's just the truth.

Hex nods and puts his hand over mine, paper over a rock, like in the hand game I used to play with Venice.

"And my brother?" I ask again. Again! "Do you know where we can find him?"

She shakes her head no, winding tresses like silken rings around her fingers. "I'm sorry, I can't see that but I see his face. Light eyes? Not blue or green, though. Almost . . . like the lightest shade of the rocks? Perhaps he's hidden himself, his psyche, as protection from others who have sight?"

Since when can Venice "hide" himself from those with second sight? (I remember: He hid himself from monsters in his *dreams*.) Since when is second sight an accepted element of the world? Since when is the world populated with giants and magical girls? Since the Earth Shaker.

But there was a question in her voice when she suggested he had hidden himself from her mind. Perhaps she can't "see" where he is for a worse reason. Perhaps he is gone. Tara said she could see living people; she never mentioned the dead. *No, he can't be. . . .*

I cover my eyes with my palms and try to breathe but it catches in my throat as if there's a wishbone lodged there. Hex holds up my cup and tells me to drink more tea.

"I don't think he's gone," Tara says, in answer to my silent terror. "I can only see his eyes, not where he is. The mother may know. Or . . . the man."

I am suddenly so tired, light-headed, calmer (from

the tea?) and I lean against Hex. His arm circles my rib cage. It feels like it's going to float away from the rest of my body. "I don't understand," I say.

I hear Hex as if from far away, for the narcotic drowsiness has overtaken me. "Please tell us more. Explain to us."

"Sleep now," she says. "Dream now. I will tell you when you awaken."

I sleep so long and deeply that when I wake, sweating, with silver-green shadows falling over my face, I can't remember where I am, or, for a moment, *who* I am.

Then Hex says my name and I recognize his face. I exist in his eyes so I exist and even the pain in my body lessens. The water outside laps the houseboat in soft insistence. It reminds me of Argos waking me with his puppy kisses so long ago it seems more ephemeral than a dream.

Ez and Ash are sitting at the low wooden table eating a bowl of something that smells warm and sweetish. The girl isn't here.

"What happened?" I ask.

"Tara went out to look for food and herbs," Hex tells me. "She thinks there may still be live plants in the hills." (I find myself listing the ones I know: *Desert lily*

*and yucca. Primrose and buckthorn and creosote and sage. Sun-
flowers and dandelions are edible. Dogbane for poison.* . . . A
mild convulsion rocks my spine thinking of the possible
need for toxic substances.) "She says she will tell us more
later. She says we have to get ready to fight."

I cover my eyes and lie back down on the small bed
where they must have placed me. The girl is crazy, don't
they see? Why must I fight? I want to run, keep running
away. Maybe some life exists beyond all of this.

But what if my mother is where Tara says she is? The
map told us to go there, too. But where is my brother? I
had more questions to ask. How had I let myself sleep?

I'm angry now—at myself, at Hex, at crazy Tara with
her visions and her live trees. I get up and look out at the
fan palms and the dark water. There's no birdsong now
but a buzzing sound in my head like mosquitoes, or maybe
there are mosquitoes left among the living. What diseases
would post–Earth Shaker insects carry? "Did she tell you
anything else?"

Hex says no. Ez and Ash were also sleeping when she
left. They offer me the porridge she made them but I'm
too upset to eat.

"You needed to rest," Hex says. "I think she gave us
the tea to restore us. I trust her. You're the one who
believes in the orange butterflies. . . ."

"Then where is she?" Again I feel like I can't breathe in the small space of the houseboat. There are no butterflies here now. "Why did she leave?"

"She'll be back," Hex says. But he doesn't sound so sure.

When Tara doesn't return after dark, an agitation possesses me, Hex, Ez, and Ash, turning us into its dancing marionettes. We break up into pairs and walk around the oasis, calling for Tara as if she's just gotten carried away looking for herbs and forgotten about us. But inside I know it isn't like that. I feel queasy and my temples thump as if my brain's trying to get out of my skull. The night is getting blacker.

Eventually we go back to the houseboat and Ez makes the rest of the porridge. I eat it, sweetened with some honey from one of Tara's jars, and it takes away the pain in my stomach. Then Ash picks up the lyre and runs his fingers over the strings, begins playing with great surety, as if he's done it always. I close my eyes, soothed for a moment by the music. It seems to change the ions in the air, makes it easier to breathe again.

"How did you learn how to play that?" Ez asks.

Ash shrugs. "I like instruments. I played piano when I was little. It's just sort of natural?"

"How little?" Ez asks, eyebrows raised.

"Maybe three? I don't know."

"A musical prodigy," says Ez.

"Yeah, just a nerdy choirboy," Ash replies.

Hex comes and lies next to me on the bed. As Ash continues to play softly, Hex reads a chapter from *The Odyssey* to us. It's the part where Odysseus ventures to the Underworld and consults with the blind prophet Tiresias who had lived seven years as a woman.

> "*'You want to know,' said he, 'about your return home, but heaven will make this hard for you. I do not think that you will escape the eye of Neptune, who still nurses his bitter grudge against you for having blinded his son. Still, after much suffering you may get home if you can restrain yourself and your companions. . . .'*"

The quote both frightens and reassures me. If we really are on a modern-day odyssey, as the parallels with the book seem to confirm, we may have the hope of returning "home" as Odysseus did. But what is home now and what if we can't "restrain" ourselves? What more will we have to endure? What do we have to prove? And to whom?

"Oy vey," Ez says. "Doesn't sound too good to me."

"Maybe this Tiresias guy was on crack?" Hex offers.

"No, he was wise," I say. "Because he understood both

genders." I squeeze Hex's hand under the blanket and he kisses the top of my head.

"Maybe because he was blind, too. It allowed him more sight. Our weaknesses are our strengths. Our flaws are our gifts." Ash says all of this, unexpectedly for our usually less-than-philosophical pretty boy, bending his head toward the strings of his instrument as if they had just whispered that information to him.

Then Hex and I fall asleep to the sounds of Orpheus's lyre, readying ourselves for our own trip below the earth.

The next morning Tara still hasn't returned. Worry gnaws at me, as hard a taskmaster as hunger. Worry for us, for her. *I missed you. I've longed for you.* Anyone who lives in this enchanted place (for the extent of its enchantment has fully hit me now that I am rested and fed) cannot be ill-intentioned. She was trying to help us, I'm sure of that now. What happened?

"I say we leave," Hex says.

Ez and Ash look at him, baby twins with their big, soft eyes.

"Don't you think we should stay here, for a little while longer?" Ez says. I can tell he doesn't want to give up the comforts of this place. None of us do but I have something more than comfort on my mind.

"No," says Hex, chin set.

"I like it here," Ash offers. "We all do, right?"

Hex ignores him; I know he thinks that, unlike Ez, Ash hasn't earned his right to weigh in yet. "Pen?"

"I have to find out if she's right about my mother. You think it's definitely Las Vegas?"

Hex nods. "Two sources told us so. But you two boys will be happy to know we can't leave for a few days. We have some work to do or it'll be the epic fail in sin city."

"What kind of work?" Ez is scraping the last bit of porridge out of the bowl, gobbling like he does when he's agitated or scared.

"I need to teach you to fight," Hex says. "Maybe Tara will be back by then."

16

MORE THAN WORDS

"YOU'RE GOING TO HAVE to get over yourself,
Pen, and learn how to kill," Hex says as we stand
on the bank of the oasis, his sword in my hands.

Learn how to kill? Not me. It's not something I can
do. I was raised in a peaceful home.

"But not in a peaceful world," Hex says when I try to
object. "It wasn't even Then."

And I do know what it's like to be angry. I used to
get so angry at Congress and the banks, the bankers
fighting with my father on the phone, the racists and
homophobes on TV, the slaughter of animals, the poison-
ing of the water and the air, the burned-through ozone,

the refusal to legislate on behalf of the helpless planet. Sometimes I'd take that anger out on my mom and my brother, the people I loved the most. But Then, during Then, I never picked up a weapon; I never harmed anyone, not even bugs. Did that mean I couldn't learn about killing, that I couldn't find it in me? Since Then, though blindly (in spite of two seeing eyes, for I kept them closed), I'd stuck scissors in a Giant's orb. And I am harder now, toughened by the days on the road. Although we haven't eaten much, the muscles in my arms and legs look more defined, and I think I move with more coordination than before. Maybe Hex's grace and power have rubbed off on me a bit.

"I'm sorry," he says, "I just can't let you back down now. I need you." He looks out across the water. "I have a feeling," he says, "that things are going to get worse."

He stands behind me, his hands on my arms as I hold his sword. He's told me the name of its parts: *shinogi-ji, hira, ha, shingo, hamon, mune, munemachi, nakago, hamachi, mei, mekugi-ana, nakagojiri.*

I can smell the chemicals and perfume of the sunblock I took from the Giant's store, activated by Hex's sweat. He is so close that I could turn around and kiss him, feel the firm/yielding pressure of his lips, but I know now isn't the time and I'm afraid he would gently put his hands on my shoulders, hold me at arm's length, and remind me of this. Better to have him close this way, even if it's for war not love. And Hex would argue it is for love, because how else can we be together when so much evil threatens us at every turn. So I let him teach me.

I know the names of all the parts of the sword but I don't know how to use the sum of them. Now my arms shake but Hex steadies me against him and I feel his heart like an anchor to which I am securely chained.

"When you strike, it is not a thought." He enunciates every syllable, speaking in the voice of a Hex I haven't met before. "It is pure action. You embody the result not the action. Like the deepest meditation."

It doesn't feel right to me to be holding something so sharp. But then I think of everything that has happened so far and I understand. I understand it as the natural outcome of what we have become. My arms and legs tingle with the Giant heaviness. Maybe I'm afraid of the sword not because I think I might fail to defend us but because I'm not so certain I won't give up and turn it on myself.

After our lesson, Hex tries to teach Ez and Ash but he decides they're hopeless and dismisses them. Ash wants to play the lyre while Ez, who has found some paints in

Tara's houseboat, spends the day painting a cornucopia, spilling with purple figs, green grapes, and overblown pink roses, on the side of the van. It's uncanny, his work—museum quality, old master quality. Even Hex has to admit it almost makes up for his inability to wield a sword.

In the evening, Hex and I go down to the shore of the oasis and he pulls off his T-shirt, exposing the inked heart and the word—*Heartless*. He undoes his belt and pulls off his jeans, stands there in black boxers, looks at me, runs a hand through his hair, steps into the water.

It's the first time we've been able to actually bathe. I care more about this, and the idea of being close to him, skin to skin, in the water, than about how I look, so I undress too, tossing my clothes aside on a rock, and step to the edge and slide in, up to my neck. The water is dark green, the color of Hex's eyes. I move closer to him. The sun is starting to set, streaming red light across the oasis. Then his hand reaches for me under the water, grasping my wrist, drawing me close. I tilt back my head and close my eyes, inhaling the scent of—what? *Quartz, garnet, cinnabar, serpentine, fluorite, wolframite, olivine, tourmaline, gypsum, hornblende.* I try to recall the names of minerals I know, wondering which ones are really here, trying to distract myself from what is happening. Because it's scary to feel this much in such a dangerous world. Even if what you feel, overwhelmingly, like inhaling the precious, still-surviving existing earth, is not fear but love.

"What's wrong?" he asks me, maybe sensing in the frantic thud of my pulse more than happy excitement.

"I haven't ever . . ."

"Because I wasn't born this way?"

"No, not that. Not that at all."

Hex says softly, "Baby, I love you. Pen. More than I love the color black. More than I love cigarettes, more than I love books. Even music."

"More than food," I whisper through our kiss, shuddering as his hands find me under the water. "More than art or stories." Then I can't speak anymore. . . . *More than words . . .*

For three days we stay here, in paradise. Tara doesn't return. *I missed you. I've longed for you.* We eat small amounts of her food. Hex teaches me to sword fight. Ez paints, insectlike flowers and petal-ish butterflies on the van. Ash plays music. In the evening I borrow one of the large bright silk scarves from Tara's closet, draping it as best I can around myself. (I was never good at this type of girlish thing, though Moira tried to teach me.)

Then I meet Hex down by the water.

As well as instructing me to use a sword by day, by night he teaches me about my body. Sensations I had only read about or imagined quake through me with the urgency of disaster until I collapse in his arms.

I grow bolder by the second evening, grabbing his hips before we're hidden under the water, hoisting myself onto him, legs wrapped around, my mouth on his neck, surprising us both.

But as we're lying on the bank under the palms— a thin piece of chrysanthemum-yellow silk our only cover—I reach for him and he gently moves my hand away.

The next night, our last one here, I beg him to let me touch him. Shy as I am, I want to see him experiencing pleasure, see the flash of incisors as his lips part for more breath. The sun is setting and the air grows chill; we'll have to go in soon. In spite of the lull of the oasis, we're never sure how safe we are here, especially after dark. I am standing behind him, my hands on his hips, my head on his shoulder.

"You don't have to. I'm fine," he says.

"But I'm not, I need it. It's for me."

"I'm not sure I'm . . . I've never felt okay that way." His voice roughens, cracks. "Like there's something wrong. That's one reason I had to get high all the time. . . ."

This vulnerability surprises me. He's always seemed so confident—with Beatrix, talking about the pretty girls.

"There's nothing wrong with you, believe me. You are the one perfect thing." As I go on tiptoe to kiss his mouth over his shoulder, I let my hand slide down his smooth-pulsing belly to his groin, and though he startles he doesn't push me off. Instead, almost involuntarily he pushes his hips forward, up against my fingers. I curl them into a soft fist and stroke him the way I used to touch myself before the Earth Shaker, when touch wasn't something you thought you'd have to do without and when love wasn't the difference between life and death. This time it is Hex, for once, who collapses in my strengthening arms.

17

DEAD SEA

W E HAVE STOCKED THE VAN with Tara's
supplies, including some cans of oil we found in
a shed. We hesitated at first but decided she would be
okay with our taking them. Now we have water and jars
of pickled vegetables and meats. They float in their brine
like strange, colorful fetuses. I'm not hungry but Hex,
Ez, and Ash savor each bite. We also have Tara's small
glass bottles of tinctures for purifying water and adding
nutrients to soil and food, but we aren't sure we trust
them yet, or that we're quite that desperate, so we haven't
tried. And we each have a knife taken from Tara's kitchen
since Hex says that's the next best thing to a sword. I
can't imagine what I would do with mine if I needed to

LOVE IN THE TIME OF GLOBAL WARMING

use it on a Giant. It is small with a white wooden handle and strange symbols etched into the sharp blade.

On the way to Vegas we stop at the Salton Sea. While Ez and Ash sleep in the van, Hex and I wander out over what appears at first to be sand but is actually—when you look closer—crushed fish bones, barnacles, and debris. Rusted cars and ruined furniture make a devil's living room. We reflexively put our hands over our noses and mouths when the rotten-egg stench of sulfur hits us in the face. The water is dark and thick with green algae, and dead fish and birds rot on the shore. Hundreds of eye sockets and mouths gape at us like creatures from a Hieronymus Bosch painting I used to have nightmares about.

"This place was a wreck even Then," Hex says and starts singing "Highway to Hell" under his breath. I wonder how many more hells we are going to have to traverse. I'm getting immune to them in some ways but I think that may be a sign of how I'm losing my soul a little each day. I was never as sensitive as Venice but the sight of an injured bird, a trip to the animal shelter, or the death of one of our pet fish used to make me cry. I think of Venice standing here, surveying the ruin, and for one second I'm glad he's gone. He shouldn't have to see any of this.

Maybe my soul has left; how else could I even think of him being gone, even if it would spare him pain? I put my hands to my thudding temples.

"No butterflies here," I say, in what might be a soulless voice.

"No," Hex replies emphatically, squinting out over the wreckage, and for a second I think he's read my mind and is telling me my soul is not yet gone.

"Why do you think there were butterflies? When I met you, Ez, Ash, Tara. What does it mean?"

"They're the souls of the dead," Hex says. "Spirit guides. Maybe your dad and mom and . . ." He stops. "I'm sorry."

"No, it's okay." Maybe my mom is dead. My dad is gone. Once again I wonder if I'm alive, because Penelope of the past could not have withstood even the idea of this. At least Hex didn't say Venice; even dead-hearted Pen could not handle the destruction of her last shred of hope. I take my new knife out of my pocket and examine the blade in the vicious red light of the setting sun.

Hex turns to me and gently takes the knife away, pockets it. This time it does seem as if he's really read my mind. "I want you to be a fighter. But I don't want you to forget who you are."

I move closer and look into his eyes where the sea is

still alive. "I'm scared," I say. It's the first time I've let myself say it.

"The true warrior isn't immune to fear. She fights in spite of it."

"That's the same for the true lover." I lean in and kiss the tattoo on Hex's neck so that my lips feel the beat of his pulse. He throws back his head and shuts his eyes. His arms circle my waist, drawing me close so our pelvises touch. I'm glad he's holding me up because my knees are collapsing with the relief of touching him again. He moves his head so our lips meet and it's like I've been given some world-changing elixir. The sulfur smell, the bones, the rotting sea are all gone. It is just Hex, my warrior lover, and me.

18

AFTERWORLD

W E'RE IN WHAT USED to be Las Vegas. The
last time I was here was with Moira and Noey
for Moira's cheerleading convention. Cheerleading: one
of the things that is hard to imagine ever existing.

*Moira went out for cheerleading in eighth grade and made the
team but she didn't realize how serious it was, that she'd be
practicing every day after school and going away all the time.
Moira wasn't what you might expect a cheerleader to be like,
except she was pretty and could dance and do gymnastics. It was
hard that year. She made new friends, girls none of us would*

have talked to before. I was relieved when she didn't try out in ninth grade. But my mom took us all to the Vegas competition because Moira's mom had to work again that weekend.

The hotel wasn't one of the fancy, themed ones; it had small rooms and bad fake gold and red velvet décor and the lobby smelled of desperation—grease, sweat, alcohol, smoke. In fact, the smell of cigarette smoke was in my sinuses all weekend. But we went to this buffet in the hotel the first night and ate all kinds of crazy junk food like Jell-O salad and cheeseburgers and fries and sodas and this pink whipped cream dessert thing and my mom didn't complain. And then we went to the competition and Noey and I screamed when Moira came onstage in her green and gold uniform, her hair and her height and her long, pale limbs (the other girls all had real or fake tans) making her stand out from the rest. The whole thing reminded me of something out of a dystopian teen novel with the flashing neon, the cacophonic music, the howling, cheesy announcer, and the girls looking like endangered prey in the pit of the arena.

That night, Noey and Moira and I ate at the buffet again and then took a Jacuzzi while my mom crashed in the room with some literary mystery novel. The sky never seemed to get dark, only to glow with a lurid haze from the strip of bigger hotels in the distance. A desert breeze rustled the skirts of the palm trees. I felt better as soon as I was in the warm churn of water with my friends, away from the rest of Moira's team.

"You were awesome," I told her.

She grinned, her head floating above the water and her glittery eye shadow starting to melt. "I'm so glad you guys are here. I'd freak otherwise."

"Let's come here again," Noey said. "When we're rich. And we'll stay in that Egyptian hotel or Paris or New York and eat sushi and lobster and drink champagne and get married at one of those chapels."

"To each other," Moira said. And my heart did a flip like a mermaid's tail.

We took the elevator back to our room and a drunken, white-haired man asked us what we were doing for the rest of the evening. Noey said, "Oh, you know, playing Barbies and eating Tater Tots," which threw him, but Moira smiled her best cheerleader smile and waved dainty fingers when we exited the elevator, the steel doors sliding closed in his face.

We were all in the same bed again that night, chilly under the thin blankets and scratchy sheets, skin and hair scented with chlorine we hadn't washed off, Moira's sharp toenails snagging, delicately, my shin in the dark.

And now I am here with Hex and Ez and Ash, and Moira and Noey are gone. I never let myself think about how they died in the Earth Shaker, if it was the earthquake or the waves or something worse. But I have also given up on imagining that they are alive. It would be almost more terrible to think that and then find out something else. Tara said she saw my mother and maybe my brother but there was no mention of my two best girls running away like nymphs across the lawn.

Las Vegas is a perfect place for Giants; everything still standing was built to their scale and now without the lights they can slumber safely and wait for prey. Ash is driving when we arrive, Ez directing him while Hex sleeps with his head on my lap in the backseat. We are always driving too fast, it seems, scared of what might reach out for us from the sky. Eventually Ash stops the van. Everywhere graffiti reads *Welcome to the Afterworld.*

I say, "Giants must love it here."

"That's the point," Hex tells me from my lap. I didn't know he was awake.

"Where should we go?" Ash asks.

I look around at all the fallen castles and arches and towers. Where would my mother be? I have no idea.

We decide we need a plan so we set up camp behind a large stack of broken Grecian columns, shattered golden Buddhas and medieval candelabras, splintered gondolas, ransacked suitcases, destroyed slot machines, and the now familiar human bones. Ash keeps watch from on top of a Louis XVI chair with torn upholstery, his lyre at his side. Hex builds a fire and Ez puts some soup in a pan to warm.

"Last can o' tomato," he says.

"Don't remind me," Hex mumbles. "I like the tomato. It reminds me of rainy days. With grilled cheese."

"I thought you only liked junk food." I punch his shoulder.

Ez wrinkles his nose at the soup and runs a hand through his red curls. "I don't remember what an actual vegetable tastes like."

"At least we have the stuff from Tara," Ash says from his post.

I prefer metallic tomato soup any day to pickled roots that look like homunculi and unrecognizable meats.

After we eat, Hex suggests we read passages from *The Odyssey* aloud for inspiration. Maybe we're stalling but it feels like we need more fortification than tomato soup, and words can do that when food is scarce. So can kisses but that doesn't seem like an option right now.

Usually Hex reads to us but he thinks we should all take a turn tonight. I ask Ash if he wants to read while I keep watch, but he shakes his head.

"It's okay. Not much of a reader." He looks out at the black sky hanging low over the rubble of a Giant's ruined playground. "My mom used to tell me how stupid I was. That I was a stupid fag and I was going to hell. I guess she was right about the hell part."

My body clenches with righteous anger at his mother and I don't know what to say to this—Ash never mentioned anything about his family before. We are all walking around with pain. I realize how little we know about one another.

Ez is silent too—he just tightens his jaw—but Hex won't let something like this slide.

"Fuck that," he says. "If all the stupid queers are so bad why are the four of us still here?"

We all laugh in a bitter way at Hex's words. It's something I wonder about almost every day—why we were spared when so many weren't. We might all be queer but stupid we are not. Still, why are we on this journey then? Maybe it's a bad idea.

Ash throws a glance back over his shoulder at Hex. "Wait, since when are you queer?"

"I am not what I once was," he answers and though Ash and Ez exchange a glance, no more discussion seems to be needed.

"Maybe we have superpowers," Ez says. "I mean, besides the basic natural queer superpower."

"My superpower is love." Hex gives me the smile that makes my body hurt with the effort of not grabbing and kissing him. "Mad skills. I can take you to other worlds, believe me."

I can vouch for that.

"What about you, Ez?" I ask.

"I have no idea. I'm a coward and a sugar addict? I don't think that qualifies me."

"You're brave," Ash says from atop the golden chair. "You just don't know it yet."

"And you're a musical genius," Ez replies. "Pen's our storyteller."

"I don't have any powers," I say. "Let alone super."

"Not true." Hex's face is lit red above the leaping flames he's brought to life. "You're still discovering them all."

"You're the god of fire," I say.

He lifts his hands above the flames as if he's controlling them. Then he says, "When the thing happened, the Earth Shaker thing . . ." He pauses. We've never talked about it before—the moment it happened, what we did, how we felt. It's been too hard to think about. But maybe we're stronger now.

"I was living at the Culver Hotel. I'd just gone to sleep after doing an apocalypse set for December 21st. Those Mayans had it going on. The flames were all around me, eating up all the curtains and the bedspread. I just stood there, like fully mesmerized, waiting for them to get me. And then it all stopped. They died down around my feet."

We are quiet, staring at Hex. I remember how he seemed to control the flames at the Lotus Hotel. He grins and I can see he's embarrassed. "Good times."

"I had something similar," Ez says softly. "I was at my parents' house, with my brother. The floor was rolling like a dragon was under it, and things were falling on me. I got down in a ball and covered my head with my hands and kept screaming, 'Stop, stop, please, Gaia, Ki, Terra, Zemyna, stop this, please listen to me, goddesses of the earth.'

"This huge bookcase was teetering. . . . I knew it was going to crush me. I closed my eyes. Then it stopped and the bookcase fell in the other direction.

"But when it was over, my family . . ."

I grab Ez and pull him close. He buries his head under my chin. "I'm sorry I snapped at you when you asked about him, when we were at the Hood sign."

"It's okay."

"His name was Eliot," Ez says. "We were identical. But he was totally different. He was brave."

Ash blinks at him with eyes like a fawn's. "I'm so sorry."

"We all lost people," Ez says, wiping his nose on his T-shirt. "I'm sorry." He addresses this to Hex.

Hex is chewing on his knuckle and I bet he wants a cigarette. I think about him by himself in his room, facing the flames, alone at dawn, no one to lose. How I wish I'd known him, Then. I think of him sitting next to me in the dining room in the pink house, holding my hand under the table while we eat burritos in mole sauce, my mom lecturing him about not drinking sodas or smoking.

"In some ways it's a lot easier when you don't have anyone," Hex says.

It's his way of apologizing. Ez nods at him, acknowledging this.

Ash squares his shoulders against the night, not looking at us. He's ripped the sleeves and lower pants legs off what Hex called his "twee suit" so he looks ragged and tough. "I was lifted up by the wind. It carried me across the desert. It carried me like I was a piece of paper and landed me inside the T-Rex."

Nothing surprises me anymore. I can see Ash flying like an angel through the desert, his ropy dreads buoying him up, arms outstretched, eyes shut.

I close my own eyes, imagining, and when I open them everyone is looking at me. "What?" I say, not meeting their three sets of irises—amber, jade, and celadon. "What?"

"Tell us," they say.

I did not part the waters. I am not capable of anything special except reading encyclopedias. I did not part the waters.

But I do remember, before I passed out, that I held up my hands to the wave that was hurtling toward the front door of my house, the part of the flood that took my father. I stopped that wave and it subsided and drifted away. I saved the pink house. I saved myself.

We are all insane. But how do you distinguish sanity from insanity, how do you diagnose abnormality in this new world?

I finish my story and we are all very silent for a long time.

"We have to forget this," Hex finally says. "We are here for a reason and it's not to think we're gods now."

But whether we are demigods or deluded children, where do we look first?

So many ruined hotels around us.

"Why don't you all rest," Ash says. "I'll stand guard."

Hex narrows his eyes. "I think you may need more than that harp thing to protect us."

Ash shrugs and with one deft hand catches all of his

dreads up in a hair band. "*Lyre*, not harp thing. Maybe not. But I'll wake you if I do."

Hex's expression says *Since when does this guy talk back*, but he lets it go. I wonder if I'll be able to sleep. Not only because I'm anxious but because the close proximity of Hex's body is causing a stirring in me like a warm breeze in the oasis fan palms. When we lie down he puts his arm around me but he doesn't touch me anywhere else and soon he's asleep. I can't get comfortable. The mattress in the back of the van is thin and I can feel the wire springs sproinging into my back. Ez, lying on the backseat, is breathing evenly, asleep, too. I can see Ash outside the window of the van, poised on the junk pile, just a shadow. He looks so vulnerable there and I wonder if this was a good idea.

I'm just drifting into a dream of Hex's hands on my body, hoping it's real, when I hear the soft rippling sounds of the lyre and I sit up. Why is Ash playing? I open the door of the van to tell him to stop—Hex will wake up and kill him for giving us away with the sound— but Ash's back is to me, his hand gesturing for me to wait. There is something commanding about him and I stay where I am and look past him to the dark beyond.

A huge, naked female figure with thick rolls of pink and white flesh is hunkered in front of Ash. A pair of pale, froggy eyes in a bemused, sagging face watch him like he is Mesmer, the original hypnotist. She seems to see nothing else. Ash continues to play the lyre, looking directly at her. He has taken his dreads out of the hair band and they blow in the wind around his face. He appears as if he might fly into the air at any moment.

I hear someone behind me and see Hex fully awake, holding his sword. I catch his eye and shake my head no. Ash knows what he's doing right now, though I may have doubted him before; this I try to psychically convey to Hex. But I don't need to. Because the Rubenesque Giantess is closing her eyes, the lids falling shut, heavily, as a child's do in entranced sleep, her whole massive body slumping.

Ash backs up, as if he's protecting us with his body, and gets into the van and spirits us away into the night.

Ez wakes and sits up in the back of the van, rubbing his eyes. "What?" he says.

Hex pats Ash on the back as he drives. "Ez, your friend just earned his keep."

19

AN EYE FOR AN EYE

WE'VE PARKED THE VAN again and armed ourselves. Walking through the city, I feel like a parade of live *hors d'oeuvres* for Giants, here for the taking in spite of Hex's sword, our knives, and Ash's seductive lyre.

I'm out of breath and need to stop. Hex gives me a sip of water from his canteen. I'm careful not to take too much; even with the supplies from Tara we don't have enough to last us very long. We left some for her, in case she came back.

No one is in the cartoony-looking medieval castle with its smashed turrets and ramparts. The half-size

Eiffel Tower lies on its side among white and pale blue plaster and crystal chandelier rubble. A green plaster Statue of Liberty is cut in half at the waist, all that remains of New York, New York (and perhaps more than what remains of the real New York).

But smoke rises from the black pyramid flanked with fake palm trees, an indication that someone is there. So that is where we decide to start.

We stand at the paws of the giant plaster sphinx. Its kohl-rimmed eyes look startled and dead at once. I lean against Hex's shoulder and close my eyes for a second, seeing small rainbow pricks of light on a black background as if I have my palms pressing to my lids. How will I be able to go inside?

Ez takes my hand; I can't tell if he is comforting me, or himself.

"What do you want most?" Hex asks softly, staring at the cracked pyramid.

"My family," I say. And you, I think.

Hex nods.

But what if my mom and Venice aren't in there, what if Tara was forced to direct us here, what if it's a trap? Still, my brother never stops crying for me in my mind.

The lobby smells like smoke, stale at best, deadly at worst. Immense gold pharaohs surround us and gold columns engraved with hieroglyphics hold up the soot-blackened ceiling. A large pile of bones in a fire pit in the middle of the gold-and-black tiled floor tells us we're probably at the right place. Hiding in shadows, keeping our distance from the red light cast by the flames, we head toward the casino.

There, Hex draws his sword and we all take our places beside him.

A Giantess that resembles the last one, except wearing an Egyptian headdress, sits still as stone, holding a slot machine in her hand like a toy. She presses the levers, staring blankly at the pictures of bright fruit and animals, ignoring us.

We pass unseen, still part of the shadows, into the café. There are three more Giants here, two males and another female, eating slabs of meat they tear from carcasses hanging from the ceiling, and slurping liquid from silver champagne buckets placed below the dripping dead animals. Drunk on blood, satiated, they don't seem to know we're here. The creatures, with their shadowed eyes and sunken mouths, and the slabs of raw meat hanging from hooks, remind me of the Francis Bacon painting I used to look at obsessively.

We pass the drunken Giants and go into a smaller room. A woman lies on a table in one of the booths. I come closer and she holds out a bony, stick-fingered hand. I feel as if I'm dreaming, walking through a thick cloud, like I can't reach her. Hex and Ez are on either side of me, Ash walks behind. I concentrate on that—that they are here, that I am not alone.

"Penelope," the woman says.

I don't let myself cry, don't want to believe it's her; the pain will be too much if it isn't.

When I used to feel pain I tried to calm myself by imagining the parts of a flower—the calyx made of sepals, the corolla made of petals, the androecium made of stamens, the gynoecium made of carpels. But you can't get rid of all the pain that easily. Once it's there it's like water traveling up from the roots of a plant through the xylem to the leaves.

The woman has on a white gown that looks like it's made out of a tablecloth and her hair is straggling around her thin face. Her head and hands appear too big for her body. Her eyes are rimmed with long lashes. And they are gray. When I was a little girl I used to think she looked like the goddess Aphrodite, whom my father read to me about from the books of myths. The glamorous bone structure, slim waist, full breasts and hips. At that time, all I wanted was to be like her when I grew up. Or, maybe, no? To be worthy of her in some strange way.

"Mommy!" I fall down next to the table, my face crumpling with the force of the realization, unable to contain the emotion any longer. "Mommy!"

"Penelope?" She is crying but her mouth is still the same. The mouth that kissed good night, whispering "I love you, I love you," so many times I couldn't count. And it didn't matter because there were always more I love you's until there weren't.

"Can you get up? I'm taking you with us," I say. "These are my friends. They'll help."

She smiles at them. "Beautiful, all of you," she says. "So beautiful in this dark place."

"Can we carry you?"

She shakes her head no. "I can't leave here, darling. Didn't they explain?"

We lift her from the table; she's so light I could carry her by myself but I don't want to. She feels like she'd break into little pieces if I dropped her. Her hands are around my neck and she looks into my face, her voice as dry as her chapped lips. "Look at your eyes."

She doesn't say anything about my tresses being gone but her hands reach for my skull and I let her stroke the short, stiff hairs.

I remember how we never stopped cuddling, kissing each other on the lips, even when I was an angry thirteen-year-old, fighting with her every day, running barefoot into the street saying I was going to find another family to live with. And that night we were in my bed together while she smoothed my hair and warmed my asphalt-pocked soles on her calves until I fell asleep.

"What happened, Mommy?" I ask. "What happened that day?"

Her lips tremble and thin to lines. "There was so much water. . . . But somehow, it didn't touch us. I don't know how. But your father . . ." She stops speaking and her eyes fill with tears again, her mouth falls open, wordless.

Daddy. With his wild hair, high forehead, the horn-rim glasses balanced on his long nose. The surfing scientist. He loved the sea, had chosen to live by the sea. How could the sea have taken him? But she said, *It didn't touch us.* She and Venice had been saved somehow.

My father's ghost fades from my mind and I see my brother standing there in his place.

"Where's Venice? Mom?"

Her hands grip tighter, stronger than you'd expect. She shakes her head and her mouth wrinkles in on itself like the little apple-head dolls we used to make in another life. "I don't know. I don't know what he did to him. . . ."

My throat is full of ash. "Who?"

"The man brought me. He knew of you. He was look-ing for you."

"What man?" I ask, already guessing the answer. There is only one man I know of who is looking for me.

"Kronen."

Hex touches me with his shoulder so I can feel the heat coming through his shirt. Kronen. Father of the Giants.

"How did he know you were my mother?"

She looks around the room, then whispers so I have to lean closer. "The walls have ears. And sight."

I think of the people at the Lotus Hotel, the sirens, Beatrix, even Tara, but I can't believe she would have harmed us.

"He was angry at us before. At your father. They worked together and your father didn't like the experi-ments he was doing. When your dad tried to expose it, his life was threatened, Penelope. We were all in danger, even Then, of more than just losing our home. I should have believed your dad." Her voice is low, confused, and mournful sounding. She reminds me of a homeless per-son, mumbling to herself on the street.

"You mustn't let him find you." Her hands dart up to my face, worrying the air around me as if trying to cast a spell of protection. I lean down to kiss her cheek, skin pale and dry and papery, crinkling over sharp bone.

And then I'm startled out of this dreamlike moment.

"It's Pen, the Giant-blinder," says a voice.

I turn to see a man, not much taller than I am. "Where are you going?" He speaks with a calm that is worse than if he had raised his voice.

"Leaving," I say. I try to sound bold but I know it's a pathetic attempt.

The man pats his goatee with his small, neat hand. "Oh no, it's not that simple. You blinded Bull, whom I created myself. One of my first two children, the ones who started it all. My baby. Haven't you heard the expression an eye for an eye?" His own eyes roll up, surveying the ceiling as he turns his hooked profile to us.

Hex steps forward with his sword drawn but then something comes out of the shadows and it is Bull, the Giant I blinded. He sniffs the air like a massive dog. The empty sockets gaping in his head reminding me of what I have done. I put my hand on Hex and pull him back.

"You must give me something in exchange for her," the man says, still not looking at us. His voice is soft, almost a lisp with his tongue.

"What do you want?"

"Fuck you," Ez says.

We all look at him. He is standing shoulder to shoulder

with Hex and I realize that Ez is quite a bit taller; I've never really thought about it before because Hex is the tougher of the two. Ez looks as ready to fight as Hex, and I wonder how this has happened.

Bull—one of Kronen's living weapons—shifts his weight. A small Egyptian statue falls from an alcove and crumbles on the floor.

"No," I say. "It's okay. Let him talk."

"An eye for an eye." Kronen is still fascinated by the ceiling, still petting the strip of hair on his chin like it's a small animal. Then he looks at me for the first time. "I want your eye," he says softly.

"What the hell. He's insane," Hex says. "Fuckin' worse than I thought, man."

But I don't care about anything except helping my mother now.

"Give me my mother and you may have my left eye," I say.

Ash and Ez and Hex all put their hands on me at once.

"Give me the eye first," Kronen says. "Or I'll have Bull take care of it."

"No, Pen," Ez says, interlacing his fingers with mine so I can feel the flow of his blood. "No!"

I turn to look at him, then at Ash and Hex. "I can't let go of her again." I want to sob but my voice is very calm.

A low growl burbellows in Bull's throat.

My mother has closed her eyes. The bones of her face jut out. She doesn't have much time left down here.

"Penelope, my hands are so cold," my mother says. "My hands are so cold. Won't you warm them?"

"Wait, Mommy. Hold on. Soon. I'll be back, I promise."

"It's too late," says Hex softly. "She won't make it."

I push my friends off of me and go toward the man. "Take my eye," I say. "I have another."

Before they can step forward, the earth shakes with the now familiar rumbles. The other Giants have come out of their stupor. They emerge from all sides, hulking over us, sniffing the air, waving their hands, blood red in the candlelight.

I know then that my eye is not enough, that my friends and I are going to lose no matter what. We are going to lose everything.

20

THE SEER

ASH WAS AWARE that it was more likely that his beauty would save him than his intelligence, which he had been told was negligible, or even his musical talents, which no one except his choral director, Luther, seemed to notice. Even the choral director was more interested in Ash's looks, anyway. The coveted lighter-than-a-paper-bag brown skin, "good" nose, and almond green eyes with teasable "girly" eyelashes, the tall, broad-shouldered, naturally muscular body.

"You should be a model," the choral director told Ash, instead of, You should be a professional singer. A musician. The choral director watched Ash all the time so that it made Ash uncomfortable, but he liked the idea of being a model someday. He thought he could do a pretty good job because he had a strong imagination (for which he was often chastised by his mother), and he had observed that the best models seemed to be able to transport themselves to other places. He could do this. He could fly in his mind. Especially when he was singing.

When Ash's mother came home from work early and found him at the one-bedroom apartment, cutting school, smoking weed, singing and playing piano for a handsome, dark-skinned boy named Darel White, she began smashing Ash's piano— the one his choral director had given him, his most precious possession, the only item he owned that made him feel like he was home. Then she called him a stupid fag and threw him out.

Ash stayed with Darel White for a few nights until his family became suspicious and asked Ash to leave. He went to the home of the choral director who lived alone in the better part of town. Luther showed his big teeth when he saw Ash on his doorstep and invited him in. That was the first time Ash was really grateful, and also ashamed, of his "good" features and lighter-than-a-paper-bag brown skin. He stayed with Luther until the night he came into Ash's bedroom. Ash went to a shelter where he lived until he landed his first modeling gig with a well-known men's magazine. Although he had been imagining it all his life, on his first photo shoot, the world ended and Ash actually flew away.

Ez was named after Ezra Pound and Eliot after T. S. Eliot, two great modernist poets. Their parents were English professors and poets so it made sense. Red-haired twins with the coloring of their Irish mother, Sean, and their Russian-Jewish father Mark's elegant bone structure. Sometimes, when he was older and had studied his namesake, Ezra wished his parents had chosen a different name because, while Ezra Pound was undoubtedly a brilliant poet, he was also known for being, in later life, a fascist and a madman.

In their white-walled, sun-washed bedroom in their rather grand, Spanish-style house that late spring morning, fourteen-year-old Ez had asked fourteen-year-old Eliot if he could tell him something. They were standing beside each other in front of the oak-framed mirror, getting ready to go to the private Westside school where Eliot excelled in sports and academics and Ez daydreamed and compulsively sketched male nudes in every class in spite of the danger of being found out. Two such different, yet identical, boys in the school uniform of white buttondown shirts and dark trousers. Ez wore a red tie, though it was not required. His hair was longer and in its natural curly state while Eliot slicked his back. This was their morning ritual, surveying themselves side by side in the mirror before they left for school. They had done it since they were very young. It was *still fascinating to them that they looked so alike and yet so different. Sometimes Ez stared into this mirror alone, thinking, I* hate you. What's wrong with you? Why don't you just go away?

Ez hadn't planned on telling his brother on this morning of this day. But somehow, staring into the mirror at the two of them, he felt compelled. That was a trait of his—compulsion. It was why he couldn't stop drawing, even when it put him in danger academically or, more significantly, socially when it was pictures of male nudes. It was why he ate too much sugar. He couldn't help it though he knew all about nutrition and even at fourteen could cook better and healthier meals than anyone in his house. He had introduced Eliot to superfoods, which seemed to have enhanced his athletic skills even more. But often, after making a meal of mung bean stew and kale salad for his family, Ez snuck off to consume a carton of rain forest–flavored ice cream, or two.

"You know, I'm gay," Ez said to Eliot's reflection in the mirror.

Eliot didn't blink an eye. "I know that, Ez," he gently replied.

"You do?"

"Uh-huh. I think most people do."

"Mom and Dad?"

"I think so, yeah."

"Oh."

Eliot turned to face Ez so Eliot's handsome profile was reflected in the mirror. "Those drawings of nude guys? Kind of gives it away. Really well done, by the way."

"Oh, yeah," Ez said. "Those."

They began to laugh, giggles at first, that turned into guffaws and then, finally, unmistakable and perfectly identical snorts. Their mother had to come knocking on the door to tell them they would be late for school.

The girl's name was Yxta. She told Alexandria that it meant princess. Alexandria thought she looked like one. A girl from a fairy tale with long white-blond braids, firefly eyes, and a soft, wan face. Even the shirt she wore was princesslike, all pink and sparkles. Alexandria had a closet full of shirts like that, most of them covered with pink sparkling hearts, and she refused to wear any of them.

Alexandria told Yxta, "Call me Lex."

Yxta and Lex. She liked the sound of their names together. The X's.

The night before Yxta came over for the first playdate Lex was so excited she hardly slept and she chewed her fingernails although her mother had made her promise she would stop that "filthy habit."

Yxta and Lex walked to Lex's big yellow and white house with the rose garden. It was just down the street from the school but Lex wasn't sure Yxta's parents would have been okay with the girls walking home alone. They had probably assumed Lex's parents or nanny walked with them but the nanny was at home, cleaning, and Lex's parents were gone, as usual. Still, Lex felt sure she could protect Yxta if a stranger bothered them.

When they got to Lex's house, the girls went upstairs to her room. It was decorated all in pink. Lex hated this but her mother had insisted. For once, though, she was glad because Yxta was delighted.

"It's a princess room!" Yxta exclaimed.

Lex shrugged. "If it was yours it would be. I'm more of a dragon."

Yxta picked up the abalone-shell-inlaid brush and looked at her friend. Lex's hair was thick, wavy, and long, although she had begged her mom to let her cut it. "I can make you into a princess, too," Yxta said. "You're so pretty."

Usually Lex did not want to look pretty but this made her stomach swirl pleasantly. She let Yxta brush the tangles from her hair and even paint her fingernails bright watermelon pink with the nail polish her mother had bought her. Even though Lex didn't like the nail polish because it smelled bad and gave her a headache, she opened the windows and didn't complain.

Yxta looked so serious, her brow furrowed in concentration and her miniature fingers skillfully applying the polish to Lex's ragged, dirty fingernails. The citrus trees in the yard and the chlorine from the pool made the room smell like summer, which it almost was.

"You have so many lemons! Can we make lemonade?" Yxta asked.

They went into the backyard and Lex scaled the tree to retrieve the best, biggest, yellowest lemons for Yxta. Then the two girls went into the kitchen and made lemonade, which they served in doll-size china tea cups.

Lex never thought anyone would ever convince her to have a tea party, let alone to sip from a doll-size cup held with pink-sparkle-painted nails. Yxta, though, had made this all seem perfectly sensible.

"See, you are a princess!" Yxta said.

"I would still rather be a dragon."

"I know. You're not a dragon or a princess." Yxta pointed to her T-shirt, which was pink, of course, and had a sparkling lavender unicorn on the front.

Lex smiled for the first time that day. She did not know that smile was even more magical than her doll-size china tea set, her mirrored bureau covered with nail polish in every shade of pink, her lemon tree, or her long wavy hair. Yes, she could be a unicorn. Their horns were sharp and could do battle.

She did not know at that time that even with a magical horn she would not be able to protect Yxta from the pills that came in almost as many shades as the nail polish on Lex's mirrored bureau. Or that, in some ways, dying from an overdose might be considered a reprieve in the world that was to come.

In my twilight sleep I can see all of them before; I know what happened to them as if I were there, watching. But I cannot see what has happened to them after we are separated, where they have gone. And I have no idea what has happened to me.

21

TWILIGHT SLEEP

WHEN I WAKE I'M LYING in an old black
Mercedes with torn upholstery, beneath a rough
blanket that smells like wet dog. Under it, my body is
iced with sweat—sleet behind my kneecaps, in the crook
of my elbows, between my breasts—that sets my teeth
chattering. There's a pain in my head like someone's been
hammering on my temples and a fierce, stitched itching
around my left eye, out of which I can't see. I reach up
and touch the cloth bandage that covers it. I try to slide
my fingers under the bandage and then I vomit all over
the blanket, like I'm puking up my heart and lungs.

"At least hurl out the window," a man's voice says.

I recognize him as the man who found me in the basement and gave me the van. Merk, who knew my parents. He takes the blanket off me and tosses it out of the car.

He's leathered from the sun and wearing a ragged shirt and jeans. His eyes watch me coolly, inscrutable.

"What happened?" I choke out the words, not really wanting him to answer.

"Kronen. You can't go back there, though. He would have killed you, slowly. I got you out in time, cleaned it up, bandaged it, and gave you something for the pain. You've been in twilight sleep."

"He promised," I say, sobbing. It makes my eye hurt more. No, not my eye, my . . . "Where is my mother?"

Merk shakes his head and looks away. "A better question is, where do you want to go?"

"Where are my friends? What happened to them? Hex!" I scream, thrashing against the sides of the car. "Hex!"

Where would they go? I think of lying with my head in Hex's lap, the houseboat rocking beneath us. I think of the two of us, swimming. His kisses . . . his hands touching me under the water the way only I'd ever touched myself before, but it was so much better. We were there together, all of us, at Tara's.

Maybe if I go to Twentynine Palms I will find her. Even though she couldn't see my brother before, maybe she will have a clue as to where he is now. Maybe she can help me find my friends.

I need to get back there. To the oasis.

I don't even realize if I speak this out loud or not but Merk says, "Yes. That's right. That's my girl."

I know the oasis has changed as soon as Merk and I arrive. I can't tell you why but I feel it in my bones and blood and in the aching empty socket of my eye. Something terrible has come here. Or perhaps it is just me, with my suffering.

Only one palm tree lies prone in the water while the others stand. The sun is setting and the water is red as if the tree is bleeding out into it.

"You going to be okay?" Merk mumbles around his cigarette.

I don't answer. It won't matter. If I say yes he'll leave and the same is probably true if I say no. He sent me off once before.

I stand by the water as the last late rays of sun burn redder, stain everything, and then fade. A cold shadow falls over the oasis, creeping chills along my arms. When the sun sets lower, no longer blinding my eye, I see the van, painted with Ez's cornucopia, parked at the other side of the oasis. Merk sees it, too.

He gives me a nod. "Go on."

"Are you coming?"

He tells me no. His eyes look strange, almost sad. "You've got to do this on your own. It's the only way to get stronger, hone your gifts."

And before I can say anything his car peels out down the road in a cloud of dust.

I run with one hand over my bandage—every step a jolt of pain—toward the van but as I approach it, I stop. Why did I let Merk leave so quickly? What if my friends aren't here? And what if someone else is?

I slither up to the windows as quietly as possible and look inside. The van is dark and empty. "Hex!" I shout, not caring if the wrong person hears. "Hex! Ez! Ash!"

My voice dissolves into the air. No one answers.

I run, now, again, toward the water and the bridge, across to the houseboat. The floor creaks as I step inside. The air still smells vaguely of herbs and desert grasses, dry and sweet. No one is here, either. I should have known.

Then on the floor I see Hex's sword.

I crouch down beside it and hold my head in both hands like it's going to fall off if I let go. Tears pour down one side of my face but the other cheek is dry as bone. The Tibetan goddess Tara was born of tears of compassion for those suffering; perhaps this Tara will appear to me now.

But no, they are all gone.

Where is Hex, his delicate hands and nostrils, his jagged smile? Where is gentle Ez and Ash who proved that we don't have to be what people tell us we are, and that lost love returns? I gave them all up. I gave up too easily. Now I must look for them, and for my brother.

I pass out on the floor, curled, like something from one of Tara's strange jars, the boat swaying beneath me and the black night lapping.

When morning comes I fill my pockets with the remaining glass vials of tinctures, take Hex's sword, and walk slowly around the oasis. The air is already burning hot and sweat weeps down my neck. Not a clean sweat but toxic and foul-smelling. As I move down toward the water to splash my face I see a small pile of something white on the shore.

It is hard to make out at first. Then I recognize some

bones of a human body (*rib, mandible, metatarsal, scapula, femur . . .*), a small human body. The bones of a girl. Sucked clean. Beside the bones lie a red silk scarf and a single silver bangle that I recognize; they once belonged to Tara.

The girl is in the low hills sloping above the desert floor, digging with a trowel among the twigs and rocks, looking for herbs and flowers, anything alive. She has faith that something is still alive besides her fan palms and the other plants in her oasis. Above her the sky is like a vast eye watching her. She's wearing her boots and jeans instead of silk scarves but there's a red silk scarf on her head, under her hat, and one silver bangle on her arm.

When she is on her knees she feels the shaking. She closes her eyes and whispers, "Om tare tam soha. I will be reborn. I will not give up on this place."

After she escapes from the monster that takes her, Tara will go back to the oasis but she will be chased down. The Giants will threaten her with death if she doesn't tell them where we are. She knows, she can see us, but she will not tell. And she will not survive. At least not in her current form.

Take my bones, Pen, bury them in the ground. Life will spring from them.

Hardly realizing what I am doing, I run, fast, back to the van, as if my speed will help in some way, as if I'm not way, way too late.

I return with the black box that once contained a map, fall to my knees, and begin to gather up the bones as if without them I will perish on the spot.

The palm trees rustle with heat, not with any breeze. My neck, bent over the box, feels so tight with pain it may snap off if I move too suddenly. I look up, at the blank sky, at the murky water. A rainbow light throbs out and then dissolves into white across the oasis. Then my one seeing eye goes black in the sun. I am falling into nothing like the rest of my world.

Venice said, "I'm so soft, you made me so soft, I don't want to be soft like you."

He had come home from school and told us that he pushed a kid.

"You know not to do that," my mom said. She was making dinner, not looking at him, that distracted, worried look creasing her face.

I went and sat with him at the table that was covered with

his Legos. There was hardly room to eat and I was mad at my mom for not making him clean it up. "Why'd you push him?"

"We were playing basketball. He was showing off and I told him he was a ball hog. He pushed me first."

My mom was finally getting it and she came over, too, wiping her hands on her apron. She smelled of onions. "You know to get help from a grown-up if that happens, right, Ven?"

"No! I don't want to tell on him! I need to show I'm not soft! Like you, all of you! Even Dad! You're all soft."

He ran out of the room and I followed him. I knocked on his door. "Please let me in."

I waited until I finally heard the click of the lock. He was sitting on the floor with hundreds of baseball cards spread out around him.

"If anyone hurts you I'll beat them up," I told him.

"No you won't."

"That's because I'm a spaz," I said.

"No, it's because you're soft."

"That's true, too."

"Dad shouldn't have lost his job," he said. "He should have fought for it."

"I don't think it's that simple."

"He should fight the bank from taking our house. He should do something."

"He's trying," I said, but I knew what Venice meant.

"I hate how soft you all are," said my brother. *His face was flushed, making his eyes appear a lighter gray, and his back was rigid. There were bruises, cuts, and scrapes on his knees but he would never complain about the pain.*

I wonder, now, as I sit in the van, how I can make up for being too soft, for not saving my family, for not saving my friends, for not helping anyone. I have a sword in my hand and I have a van and supplies. I have a black box that once only contained a map and that I filled with what I am sure are the bones of a magical girl. I even know where to find Kronen.

There is a piece of paper in the van. It says *Bank of the Apocalypse* and there are directions. It says *Find Pen. Find Kronen and kill!!! Find Pen.* The writing is Hex's graffiti scrawl.

My baby brother would never call Hex soft. Not Hex.

And not me, either. Not anymore. Not any fucking more.

22

BANK OF THE APOCALYPSE

THE BUILDING HAS GOLD COLUMNS and a massive doorway, a mural depicting Giants, with bodies sticking out of their mouths like limp cigarettes. Someone besides me has studied their Goya. *Bank of the Apocalypse* reads a handwritten sign. It balances atop a pile of ruin-rubble and clean-sucked human bones. I can make out doors and windows, crumbled fireplaces, tiles, metal pipes, shingles, signs that read *Foreclosure*. The homes of so many skeletons. People who used to fight over the last blueberry muffin at the breakfast table, get down on their knees to scrub bathroom floors, and kiss one another good night, thinking they were at least relatively safe. Now they are just dust in the debris.

I climb through the rubble toward the door. It takes a long time, time enough for a Giant to see me from the blood-red stained-glass eye window and reach out to crush me in his hand the size of a tractor.

My mother never foresaw this danger. She was scared we would get sick from drinking tap water, eating genetically modified fruits and vegetables, even breathing the air. We had to put on sunscreen every day because of that hole in the ozone that kept her up at night. She gave us vitamins and bought us only chemical-free shampoo, even though it never made my hair as soft and clean as Moira's. I used to hate how afraid my mom was and how afraid she had made me. Now I understand but I can no longer be like her. I have to fight.

The ceilings are so high I can't see the top of them, and the only light is from the red glass eye. All around me are vaults that look like crypts. The whole place is a mausoleum.

"Here she is," a voice says.

Not a Giant, but Kronen emerges from the shadows, wearing a carefully constructed suit made of patches of dried, bumpy material. I force myself to stand my ground. The sword in my hand looks like a needle, even

to me, though Kronen is only a few inches taller than
I am.

"You've come back?" he says, smiling. It further distorts the uneven planes of his face. "I knew you would
come back."

"I want my friends," I say. "You have my eye. You took
my mother. I want to know what happened to her, and to
my friends. And my brother."

"Friends are important. Brothers are important.
Sons, sons are important."

"I know," I say. "I'm sorry for what I did. But you had
your revenge. An eye for an eye."

"What will you give me if I don't help you find them?
A *stick* in the eye?" he muses.

I won't let my hand go to the empty socket hiding
under the patch. I won't think of how that eye is gone,
how it is as if every work of art, every beloved's face it
ever reflected, has vanished with it. If I saw madness in
Kronen before, now it has exploded like a boil. That
nasty suit—it looks like it's made of dried skin.

"If you don't tell me, if you don't return them to me
safely, I will kill you," I say.

Kronen pets the strip of hair on his chin in a way
that feels too intimate, almost sexual. His eyes roll up
in contemplation. "I don't know where your friends

are," he says cheerily. "Your dear mother died of natural causes, poor thing. Your brother got away from me." Then his voice changes, deepens, his eyes stab at my face. "And you could not kill me if you tried. Have you forgotten who I am? What I have made? What I have destroyed?"

His laughter turns into shaking and the shaking comes from the steps of the Giant entering the room.

Now my sword really is a needle. And the color of fear dripping through my veins? Like our old friend, Homer, said, fear is green.

"This is Kutter," Kronen says. "My other son. My perfect son. My other original. Like Bull. My babies from whom all others originated in lesser, more imperfect forms. But Kutter is the most perfect of all. I believe you have met before."

This Giant has two eyes and does not have a mistress controlling his actions. He is bigger than Bull and Frakk and looks like Kronen, with the same hooked nose and strip of hair down his chin. His eyes even roll in the same way. He's the one from the Lotus Hotel.

I hold out the *nihonto*, remembering what Hex told me. *When you strike, it is not a thought. It is pure action. You embody the result not the action. Like the deepest meditation.*

But my sword would not even scratch this monster.

Kutter stoops and examines me the way I might have once looked at an insect on a leaf. He reaches out his hand and I am entranced by the nail beds, white with fungus like an infected tree. A smell comes from his flesh, fetid and deadly, something made, but not by Gods or Nature.

"You blinded Bull," Kutter says. Now I'm not an insect but something venomous he wants to kill.

"Yes. I was trying to save my life. I have sacrificed my eye as retribution."

I pull off the bandage, showing whatever horror lies beneath.

Kutter moves closer to see, his rank breath on my face. I refuse to flinch. His eyes grow glazed, staring. I see myself reflected in his irises—two young women, each with a single eye and a dark gash where an eye once was. I think of Frakk bewitched by Beatrix's story, the Giantess mesmerized by Ash.

"And I have something else for you," I say. "Besides the eye your father took. A story about you."

"What do you know of me, little blind thing?" Kutter's voice makes the walls of the Bank of the Apocalypse shake.

"I know of many things," I say. "Gods and monsters, transformations, spells and enchantments, trees and oceans, hospitality, loyalty, betrayal, great wars. I know of *kleos* and I know of love."

Kronen laughs again, a small tittering sound. "Love? This is not a world for love." He covers his mouth primly with his hand and rolls his eyes to regard the ceiling. His suit crackles. His laughter stops. His voice deepens. "Kill her, Kutter."

The monster looks at Kronen, then turns his head to me. He blinks his eyes. I hadn't seen the sorrow in them until now.

"I will hear," he says, his hand holding Kronen back by the scruff of his neck. "Tell."

I close my eyes. I am the visionary, the one-eyed seer, the storyteller. I am Pen. I can fight with the power of images and words. "I will tell you a story of Then."

Once there was a small boy named K. with big dark eyes, a boy with the innocence of any other boy. But this boy was different in that he was too intelligent for this world. It did not understand him. At five he could do mathematics like a fifteen-year-old, at fifteen he could do college-level math and so his mother (his father was gone) enrolled him in a university. He was smarter and younger than everyone and didn't like to speak to others or to be touched. He stayed in his room and did experiments of a strange kind.

Eventually he dropped out of college, for he knew more than all of his professors, got a job in a lab and an apartment of his own.

Because he was small himself and had grown up in a small and crumbling apartment, while most people he knew lived in big houses, he wanted his beings to be huge, as big as mountains. He took the cells from the largest humans he coul' find and injected them into three embryos which he had st from the lab he worked for. Two sons and a daughter. T ildren were born and continued to grow and grow. They be hidden. They had to be operated on and undergo treatm ts so their bones would not grow too big and too weak to support their huge frames. Then K. took cells from his children and injected them into the cells of other embryos to create clones. He did not worry these would turn against him. They were his children after all, in spite of what he had done to them, how he had made and distorted them for his purposes. A very large investment company hired K. when he went to them and told them what he had created. He had faith that when they realized how much power he could help them attain, they would not betray him. They did not.

As K. grew older, he moved to a golden mansion with marble floors and built a huge laboratory. In his lab there was another scientist, who began to question what K. was doing. The scientist didn't find out everything but he knew too much and lost his job. He went home to his family in their pink house by the sea and told them what had happened, but not why. Soon he could not make payments on his house and the bank that funded K.'s experiments threatened to take the scientist's home away.

K. didn't care about the scientist or anything else; he was busy creating his race of great beings. But the problem was, the creatures grew too big. They were too big for this earth. These Giants grew so big they made the earth shake and crack.

Only some people survived the earthquake and the waves that followed. The Earth Shaker. And many of those survivors were eaten alive by the Giants who needed to feed. They also ate anything edible that grew until the available food supply was depleted.

A small band of friends survived. One of them was a young woman, the scientist's daughter. She had accidentally blinded one of the Giants. When she and her friends arrived to rescue the scientist's wife from K., he said no, he wanted something in exchange. He wanted her eye. This she gave him. She let him cut it from her face. But he did not give her back her mother as he promised. She has returned to claim her brother and her friends.

So now you know, Kutter, the tragic story of your birth. A story devoid of love. And love is the birthright of everyone. Even now. Is it not?

"How do you know this?" Kronen gasps. It's the first time I've heard real emotion in his voice; he sounds like an agitated child. "How do you have such visions?" He speaks to Kutter now: "She must be killed. Rip out her other eye and then kill her!"

Kutter tears his gaze away from me, wincing, like he's ripping a bandage off raw skin, and turns on Kronen, flexing his meaty hands.

I am not a hero, I am not Odysseus, there are no gods or goddesses guiding me. All I have is myself. And Hex's sword.

That is when I turn to Kronen and like the deepest meditation I strike and embody pure result. I embody death, not peace. The only choice in this world we have made from our betrayals and our weakness and our greed.

Kronen collapses to the ground.

Kutter waves his hands around his face like they're on fire. He stamps his feet, moaning, and the walls of the Bank of the Apocalypse shake as if about to collapse. There are tears pouring from his eyes, soaking me, and this is what terrifies me the most, to see a monster feel. I think, *Now he will kill me. Stories and visions mean nothing.*

But instead, Kutter turns and lumbers out of the Bank

of the Apocalypse. The far wall crumbles, collapsing before my eyes, glass and plaster exploding everywhere.

And someone grabs me.

It is not Hex, Ez, or Ash as I had expected, as I had wanted with every neuron (soma, dendrite, axon), with every electrical impulse that together fires up this being I think of as me. It is not Hex, Ez, or Ash who says, "Pen! Penelope! Come now! Come with me!" and lifts me onto his back and carries me out of the Bank of the Apocalypse.

It is Merk.

In the Mercedes, speeding away, I look at my hands. Blood has splattered them, splattered my clothes. Kronen's blood. The smell that never leaves me, that smell of blood, embedding itself blackly in my nostrils again.

"Good fighting, there," Merk says. "You okay, samurai?"

I stare at him. His calloused hands on the steering wheel. His rough, vagabond face now half-hidden in a beard. His thick biceps and thigh muscles. Who is he? Why is he here?

"I don't know," I say. "I have to find Venice." I realize I'm screaming and I can't stop. "Why do you keep following me?"

"Settle down, kid."

"Settle . . . Why do you even talk to me? Why are you here?"

Merk turns to me and I see his eyes and I know them and I am afraid to know.

"I knew your mom and dad, before you were born," he says. "We went to school together. College. Your mother was a fantastic painter. She . . ."

"So what? What does that have to do with anything?"

"Penelope."

"Why are you using that name? That's not my name."

"It was, Then."

"Stop it!" I scream, covering my ears with my hands so the blood rushes like an ocean.

Merk slams on the brakes so I fall forward against the dash. "I loved her, okay?" he says.

"Who? Loved who? What are you talking about?"

"Grace. Your mother. We were together. We had a child." His voice rises with emotion for the first time.

"What?"

"You're my daughter."

I want to stick my sword into him and feel the split of flesh and the spurt of blood. It would serve him right. He sent me from my home, saying it was for my safety. Because of him I blinded Bull and was pursued by

Kronen. Because of him I lost my mother and my eye and now Tara and my friends.

I look away and dig my nails into the fleshy parts of my palms.

"What do you want to do now?" he asks, and his voice is hoarse as if he's trying to control some rush of feeling.

I don't know what might come out of my mouth, what I want to do, how he can help. The world swirls around me. And then, falling through the darkness of my mind like Dorothy's house in the tornado, I see a small pink structure. "Take me home," I say.

On the way Merk tells me a story and I have no choice but to listen. Unless I try to outshout him or jump from the moving car. But I have to get to the pink house, even if nothing more of it exists.

Merk was in college with my mom and dad at Berkeley. The men had already bonded over a particular band on the first night when my mom walked into the dorm dining room with a shock of black-dyed hair and kohl eye makeup like an Egyptian queen. I'd seen old pictures of her resembling her favorite singer Siouxsie Sioux.

Merk, my dad, and my mom ate every meal together and went into San Francisco to see shows on the weekend or drove back to L.A. to hang out in Venice and surf.

"At a gig in Berkeley, Grace and David got together," Merk said. "It was always this tense balance to see who it would happen with first. We both were so in love with her. She was gifted and gorgeous. But I backed out. I could tell it was serious with them and I've never been one to settle down anyway. We stayed close through grad school. Then right before they got married your mom and I . . . It was the only time, I swear, we had too much to drink, lost our judgment . . . and she got pregnant. We told your dad right away."

It was a rainy night in their Venice bungalow, the palm trees, banana plants, and birds of paradise thrashing around like drunk kids at a concert. My dad ran outside before my mom and Merk could stop him.

"I knew he was going to the beach and that he was in danger so Grace and I went after him. I went in and pulled him out of the water," Merk told me. "He would have died. I still don't know if he was trying to kill himself or not."

When Merk and my mom got my dad back and he recovered from the shock and pain of the news, he said he couldn't have Merk around ever again. My father said he was willing to forget what happened, do what was right by my mom and raise me as his own but that Merk could never be a part of our lives.

"You rescued my dad? How did you know where he was? What do you mean you knew he was going to the beach?"

"Like you do," Merk says. "Like you know things. Since your eye."

Did I get this from Merk, the ability to tell Kutter's story, to see my friends' childhoods, to know things I couldn't know? But my sight only really came to me after I lost my eye, as if that brought it on.

"Why did you come to me now?" I ask Merk, looking out at the ruin around us.

"Because I always stayed in touch with your mom about you, through e-mail. I never came to see you because I'd promised David. And it turned out, then, that I was hired by Kronen's company. When your dad got fired for trying to expose what Kronen was doing I became 'involved,' let's say."

"What do you mean by *involved?*"

Merk's dark, fevered gaze won't meet mine. "I was supposed to keep an eye on him. Make sure he didn't talk. After the disaster, Kronen sent me and a crew to look for your father. But I went to help you escape. You were in my mind and I knew you were alive. I can't explain it; sometimes I just know. I owed you and David, big time. I'd almost ruined his life twice." Merk winces slightly, shifting in his seat, and grips the steering wheel. "I was pretty far north and the roads were a mess. Some situations came up on the way. It took me longer than I'd thought to get to you."

But he did get to me and saved my life. The father who raised me could not have passed on the killing gene. But Merk could have, oh yes. And although my story helped me, it didn't destroy my enemy. Maybe the ability to kill is all I have left.

When we get to what used to be my street, Merk stops the car.

"Are you going to come with me?" I say. I've let him leave me twice before. I want to at least tell him that I need him now.

"No, sorry. I'm only here to help you when you really need it. It's the only way you'll grow into your gifts."

"You sound like a clichéd fantasy movie." I look at the wrecked landscape outside the car. "When I really need it? You think this isn't hard enough? And what gifts? That's just BS."

"No, it's not. You know it's not. I heard that story you

told back there. You didn't just make it up. It came through you. I know because I have abilities of my own.

"And there's more, right?" Merk continues. "Something that happened when the shit hit the fan. Otherwise you wouldn't have survived."

I weave my fingers in my lap, not meeting his eyes.

He means how I stopped the wall of water.

"Pen?"

Finally I look up and see something rising out of the gloom at the edge of the sea. It's painted pink, which makes no sense beside the rest of the landscape; I think of Dalí's rose in the desert, I think of Homer's dawn. It's a dollhouse grown huge. It's a Giant's toy. It's mine.

"Please, come with me." I have no choice but to say it plainly to Merk, to beg him.

He shakes his head. "You stopped the water, Pen. You're strong. I'll be back someday, if you need me. But for now I think what you really need is right ahead of you."

He aims a finger gun at the house.

What does he mean? What I really need?

"Merk . . ." I say, afraid to go, afraid to have it not be what I need it so much to be. Whom I need it to be . . .

"Go ahead," Merk says gently, enfolding me with his voice. "Go. You don't need me now. You picked exactly

the right place for me to take you. If you hadn't picked it,
I'd have brought you here anyway. I'll unload your things
on the porch."

There is one person I need the most. I get out and I
run to my house.

23

HOUSE OF THEN

NOW THAT LOVE HAS BEEN taken from me so many times (my mother, my father, my brother, Argos, Moira, Noey, Ez, Ash, and Hex, my great-and-noble-hearted Hex) I don't know why I believe in coming here. But, somehow, I do.

There was a painting from 1890 by an American artist named Edwin Romanzo Elmer. He painted his nine-year-old daughter Effie in front of their house under a lilac tree, a sheep and a kitten, a wicker pram with a baby doll. He and his wife sit in the background, dressed in black, while Effie stands in front glowing with sunlight. The clouds in the sky look as if they are made of brick because the white paint cracked over time. It appears to be a lovely if slightly weird pastoral scene, until you learn that the painting is called *Mourning Picture* and that it was created after Effie died.

I feel like Effie returning to my house, returning from the dead. But unlike her I'm afraid I'll find that everyone I loved has given up waiting and gone to the Afterworld without me.

Houses are not homes. My father—maybe not my biological father, but my father all the same—told me that when he thought we would have to move. We never had to because foreclosure—a small disaster—was replaced by a much bigger one. We lost both our house and our home anyway. We lost each other and I know now that is all that ever mattered.

But still this house by the sea, this house with its implacable façade (very much like the one in Elmer's painting), its broken windows, and its ruined salt-encrusted yard (once there were purple morning-glory trumpet blossoms, once an acacia tree with pink flowers; there were sunflowers and citrus trees and vegetables), reminds me of what was before, reminds me of Then. I want to go inside and find my old room and lie down and dream this world away. I don't care who else has occupied the place, what marauders have decimated it. I think that at least, at last, I will reclaim my land. I have faith, at least, in this.

And more so because of the orange butterfly. I hold out my arm. It alights there, fanning its wings as if it has landed on a flower, on a sunny day, on a living planet. It stays on my arm, ticklish and fragile as a breath, as I go forward.

With Hex's sword at my side, the box of what I believe to be Tara's bones in my hands, and the butterfly now flying before me, I walk over ground that is dry and cracked in places, saltwater marshy in others, toward the front door. It's unlocked and inside it seems terribly quiet. I hear no boot steps, no breaking glass or shouting. Instead of the smell of territorial urine and fear-sweat I smell the saline winds that have blown through, blown it clean.

I go up the narrow stairs slowly, unafraid, accompanied by my winged companion. I hold my sword to defend myself only until I reach my attic bedroom. Then it doesn't matter if I die.

Dried leaves cover the creaking floorboards, becoming dust. I wonder if there will ever be new leaves, new life.

In my hands, the box of Tara's bones seems to be telling me something.

For what if I bury them in the ground outside this house? Would my acacia tree bloom? My father's vegetable garden with carrots, pumpkins, tomatoes, and snap peas?

I imagine him walking down the hall toward me in his dirty jeans, a bunch of carrots ripped freshly from the ground dangling in his dirty hands, feathery leaves and wrinkled orange roots that tasted so sweet. I sneered at them—stupid me. My mouth is a wasteland now, carrotless, despairing. I say to the air, all I have of my father's ghost, "I'm sorry."

My father taking a bite of carrot. My mother saying, "You'll appreciate what we have here one day, Pen. It's better than you think."

My brother saying, "Yeah, Penelope. Why don't you appreciate anything?"

"Why are you so annoying?" I reply.

My brother crying. How could I have made him cry? He smelled like sunshine and yellow flowers and strawberries. He smelled like a world that is now gone.

Inside my torso it feels like a landslide of dry shale where nothing will ever grow again. Time to die. I am at the door of my room but the butterfly flies off down the hall. I hear something coming from the room next door, from behind the door where the butterfly circles as if trying to get in. My heart tumbles down a secret staircase inside my chest and lands hard in the pit of my stomach.

I go toward the door and put my hand on the antique knob my mother chose so carefully. The house around me grows still as the breezes stop and the leaves on the floor rustle no more.

Inside this room, the room where my brother once lived, a boy lies on a mattress. He is wrapped in a blanket and his hair has grown past his shoulders. Out of the blanket jut his limbs that are so thin. Dirt covers his face. I see his eyes, though, clearly, gray and hallowed as the eyes of the goddess in the old lore. A dog, skinny as a stick figure, pokes his snout out of the blanket and hobbles toward me.

A small orchid in a porcelain container is sprouting tiny green whorlies of leaves. The room is full of butterflies and my butterfly joins them, becomes lost in them. Hex said that he thought the butterflies were souls of the dead, perhaps my father, my mother, guiding me.

"Penelope?" the boy whispers. And I go to him; I go to meet my brother, to take him in my arms where the space he left has never closed.

24

LITTLE GREEN

MY BROTHER ESCAPED Kronen and the Giants. In the midst of the Earth Shaker it felt like a hand had lifted him and my mother up and carried them out of the water.

"It couldn't have been a hand, we knew it couldn't but then we saw it, the Giant thing," Venice says. "It was going to . . . it almost . . . But then it saw other people running and it dropped us and chased them instead." His voice has the high, strangled tone he used to use when he told me his nightmares.

Venice and my mother ran for miles until they were caught by another Giant and taken to Las Vegas. My brother wasn't sure why Kronen kept them alive, except that he said something about luring me to him after I blinded Bull.

Venice was able to escape on foot. "I hid myself," he tells me, "with my mind," and I remember how he said he did that in his bad dreams, using his mind to hide from the monsters. That's why Tara couldn't see him. But in spite of this, Venice was taken in his sleep, when he finally collapsed from exhaustion among the ruins of a small chapel on the outskirts of Las Vegas, and was driven to the pink house by a mysterious stranger. Merk.

At first Venice thought he had died and this was the Afterlife. When he realized he was still alive he began to hope that, somehow, I would come to find him. It was not me who came, though, but Argos. He arrived two weeks ago, limping, starving, but with lights still in those black eyes when he saw my brother. At first Venice thought he was hallucinating from hunger. They've been living on a small supply of canned food and bottled water Venice says appeared on the porch a few days after his arrival.

"What happened to Mom?" Venice asks, huddling with his head between his knees so his voice is muffled and I can barely hear him.

My hands stroke the jagged blades of his shoulders through his dirty T-shirt and my throat burns with the words I say to him. "She died, sweetie."

"Dad died, too," he tells me.

"Yes." I don't want Venice to see me cry now.

He peeks up, and smooths out, with his small but still sturdy hands, the large map on the floor beside him. Another map of the world. It is large and it has almost all been colored in except for our state. "I made it for you. I've been working on it for a month, since I got here. I knew you'd come back before I finished it."

"You were right."

We survey it together, the jigsaw puzzle of ocean and land.

"Did everyone die?" Venice asks, pleading with me to give him an answer that does not send him hurtling out into the stratosphere.

I kiss the top of his head. His hair is greasy and his neck crusty with dirt. I want to tell him about Ash and Ez and especially Hex. Hex who taught me to fight and love, who held me against his chest that said *Heartless* but never was. Someday I will tell Venice about them. "Not everyone. We're here. And Argos."

At the sound of his name my dog licks my face and follows the orange butterflies with his eyes.

"And them," I say, and point to the butterflies. "They're still here."

"Why?" Venice asks, lifting his head. His eyes are red but he's holding the tears in. Brave. I used to wonder if he felt too much pressure not to cry and if that was bad for him. My parents never said not to but he learned it on the school playground, on the baseball field. When he'd be up at bat I'd pray that he wouldn't strike out and if he did I'd turn away, not being able to see him run off with his head lowered, biting his lip. I knew he was telling himself: *Don't cry. Boys aren't allowed.* They will be, now, in this new world. I wanted to tell him it was okay to let the tears flow. "Why are the butterflies still here?"

"I don't know. But we're here and we have to keep fighting. Maybe there are other people out there, too. We can't give up now."

His hand goes up to my face and I remember my bandaged eye. How it would terrify him if he saw.

"What happened?"

"I'll tell you sometime, later. It's all right. I have another."

"Does it hurt?"

"No, I don't even think about it now. I can see you, that's all that matters."

I stroke his cheek and he blinks at me, then looks

out the window into the falling darkness. "Who are those things, those monsters? They're here, too. Why are they here?"

"That man, Kronen, created them somehow, genetically engineered them."

"How?"

I remember how Venice's questions used to irritate me—so many questions, the ones whose answers he knew and the ones he didn't—and now I want them, all of them. "I don't know exactly. He changed their chromosomes and then cloned them, I think."

"He said something about Dad."

"Dad worked for him. He tried to stop him. That's why Kronen hated us. Even more when I blinded one of his Giants. But Kronen's gone and I think we are safe from them. I don't think they'll hurt us anymore."

"Are you sure?"

"No, but I don't think we have to worry about that."

There's a pause. Then, "Penelope!" He grasps my arm. "What will we eat?"

His supplies are almost gone and I only have a small amount from Tara and Merk. Not enough to last us very long. I hadn't even thought of that when Merk dropped me off.

I pick up the box of bones I've laid beside us on the

floor. I look at the orchid with little green leaves on a stalk that otherwise appears dead.

"Did you see this?" I ask him.

"Yes, it's growing. I don't know how. Can you eat orchids?"

"Have you taken care of it?"

"I found water outside," Venice says. "Some kind of spring. I'm afraid to drink it but the plant likes it."

"I have an idea," I say.

We go into the shed behind the house. It smells of decay and mold. But packets of vegetable seeds and potting soil are still there among the ceramic pots and garden tools. I guess the men who came with Merk didn't think there was a chance anything would ever grow again.

"Show me the water," I say.

Holding shovels and spades and the seed packets, Venice and I go around the side of the house and he points to the ground. Among a cluster of rocks a thin sheen of water—not stagnant, but fresh—bubbles up from the earth.

We get down on our knees and dig, the way we used to when our dad made us garden with him on weekends.

"What are these?" Venice asks when I open the box.

"Bones. Of a girl named Tara."

"She died?" His eyes are big with sorrow.

"Yes. But she'll come back," I say, not knowing why the words come out like that.

"How?"

"I don't know. But she will."

I remember how Venice used to believe in Santa and the Easter Bunny. Even when it was obvious that our mom and dad stuffed the stockings, ate the cookies, drank the milk, hid the jellybean-filled plastic eggs. I was always trying to catch them at it when I was younger, but Venice never questioned them, or if he did, he always accepted their silly answers (*Why did the Easter Bunny use eggs from our garage? He has the same ones, sweetie!*), his eyes flooded with wonder then, instead of sorrow. He wanted to believe.

In the same way, Venice nods now and when I look into his eyes I believe what I've said even more. I believe in death and destruction now, but also in magic. For I have seen all of it.

We bury the bones with the seeds in the earth, and water them from the spring, adding a few drops from Tara's glass vials. I wish, along with the plants, that my friends would grow up out of this earth in the night. As a benediction I recite some lines I remember from *The*

Odyssey when Odysseus returns and gets his father, Laertes, to recognize him.

> "...*We went among the trees, and you named them all and told me what each one was, and you gave me thirteen pear trees, and ten apple trees, and forty fig trees; and so also you named the fifty vines you would give. Each of them bore regularly, for these were grapes at every stage upon them, whenever the seasons of Zeus came down from the sky upon them, to make them heavy.*"

Venice and I go inside and share a can of fruit cocktail that Merk left with my supplies on the porch. We split a can of tuna with Argos. Then we all lie down on the mattress and I sing a song my mother used to sing to me as a lullaby; it's called "Little Green." Venice falls asleep.

Venice has always had a better sense of time than I do. I gave up trying to mark the days after the loss of my eye but my brother's kept a careful record since the Earth Shaker, except for the time he was being driven to our house. According to his estimate, it's the first day of the month of May.

In the morning I try to make this half-dream state

last, imagining the two of us sitting at the wooden table with my mother and father, Moira and Noey, Ez and Ash and Hex. Argos is poised on his haunches begging for food or lying on his back, tapping his front paws together like a seal in a circus while Moira rubs his belly with her bare foot. Venice is building a tower out of Legos and beside him sits Ez who is helping make it into a skyscraper by adding layers of figures holding hands. My dad is telling Noey about the vegetables he picked for the salad, how the cucumbers are wrinkled looking but very sweet. There are other foods, too, maybe yam and sage gnocchi or Indonesian lemongrass enchiladas.

Ash is asking my mom what's in the butternut squash soup.

"Just vegetables," she says. "Squash, carrots, yams, onion, and a bit of olive oil. The secret is to blend it!"

Hex is next to me, his bony knee wearing through the fabric of his black jeans and touching mine under the table. After dinner we're going to read *The Odyssey* together under the swirled glass amber and blue shade of the antique Tiffany lamp. Then we'll climb up the stairs to my attic room, get in bed under the old master prints, and kiss ourselves into oblivion, but only until morning. Then we will come back to the world.

I close my eyes again.

Now it is just me and Venice and Argos but perhaps someday Hex and Ez and Ash will come to join us here. If I have found my gray-eyed brother among all this devastation, anything can happen.

Something stirs against my face like fallen petals in a warm desert breeze. Orange butterflies have flown back into the room. They circle my head and then move to the window. I get up from the mattress and go to the spiderweb-patterned glass; I look out at the garden and see, among the brown and gray, something green.

Calling for Venice to follow, I run downstairs and out the front door where I fall to my knees, Argos beside me, wetly nosing my arm. Green shoots are pushing forth from the earth. Shy and sly and fresh. And I realize, things grow here. Impossibly (though what is impossible or possible anymore?) this is a place where things grow. Venice kneels, too, and puts out his hand to touch the fragile seedlings. He looks at me, trying not to show his teeth in a smile, head slightly cocked to the side, the way Argos sometimes does.

"Is it magic?"

"Yes," I say. "Real magic. Life."

Then Argos pushes up off his haunches, stands poised and quivering on his short legs, looking toward the horizon, as his nose savors the air. His tail is wig-wagging back and forth like a flag.

"Penelope?" Venice says.

I look, too, squinting with my single eye to bring the image into focus. Three figures are approaching us through the fog. A tall one with brown dreadlocks, a redhead, and a slight person with a shock of black hair as dark as the ink of the tattoos that tell his story. They stop for a moment. Then they run through the wasted land with outstretched arms, toward the pink house, toward us.

ACKNOWLEDGMENTS

This book could not have been written without the input, help, and inspiration of my assistant and friend, Jeni McKenna. I am grateful to the wonderful Christy Ottaviano for her impeccable editing skills and her support, to her Holt team: Amy Allen, George Wen, April Ward, and to Neil Swaab for the cover art, and to my brilliant agent, Laurie Liss at Sterling Lord Literistic. Rand Paulin and Jeni McKenna helped with the scientific research regarding cloning. The term "girlist" is borrowed from Leah Case as are some of Noey's photos. Hex's tattoo phrase appears in my favorite book, *House of Leaves*, by Mark Z. Danielewski. Oh, and thanks to Homer, of course!

FRANCESCA LIA BLOCK

Nicolas Sage Photography

What did you want to be when you grew up?
A writer and a fashion designer.

When did you realize you wanted to be a writer?
First grade, if not birth.

What's your favorite childhood memory?
My dad holding baby me above the piano and playing notes with my toes.

As a young person, who did you look up to most?
My mom.

What was your favorite thing about school?
Writing.

What were your hobbies as a kid? What are your hobbies now?
Writing, dancing, running, skating, reading. Writing, yoga, running, reading.

Did you play sports as a kid?
Is writing a sport?

What was your first job, and what was your "worst" job?
Cutting up vegetables at a '70s restaurant with a unicorn on the sign.

What book is on your nightstand now?
The Iliad.

How did you celebrate publishing your first book?
Crying for a few hours.

Where do you write your books?
At my desk in the "dining room" of my house.

When was the first time you read *The Odyssey*?
My dad told it to me as a bedtime story when I was very young.

What compelled you to set the story in Los Angeles?
She's my home and muse.

What can readers expect from the sequel, *The Island of Excess Love*? No spoilers please!
Pen and friends are chased from their home and confront beauty and terror on a mysterious island.

What challenges do you face in the writing process, and how do you overcome them?
Writing is the one easy thing in my life. Ask me how I overcome the challenges of my daily life and I'd say, love and writing a lot.

Which of your characters is most like you?
Weetzie on a good day; Witch Baby on a bad one. Echo every day.

What makes you laugh out loud?
My dog. Daily.

What do you do on a rainy day?
What rainy days? I'm in L.A.

What is your favorite word?
Numinous, but sometimes I forget the exact definition, so, maybe, *love*?

If you could live in any fictional world, what would it be?
Not Pen's world. Maybe Weetzie's. Narnia's kind of great, too.

What's your favorite song?
"Breathe Me" by Sia, "Ready to Start" by Arcade Fire, "Good Fortune" by PJ Harvey, "Lust for Life" by Iggy Pop, "Winter" by Tori Amos, and "Oh Very Young" by Cat Stevens.

Who is your favorite fictional character?
Atticus Finch from *To Kill a Mockingbird*.

What was your favorite book when you were a kid? Do you have a favorite book now?
It was *The Animal Family* by Randall Jarrell. Now, I'd say *One Hundred Years of Solitude* by Gabriel García Márquez, but there are so many.

SQUARE FISH

If you were stranded on a desert island, who would you want for company?
My children and some books.

If you could travel anywhere in the world, where would you go and what would you do?
Italy—to walk, eat, go to museums, and read in a pink villa.

Do you ever get writer's block? What do you do to get back on track?
With a last name like mine, I pretend that concept doesn't exist.

What do you want readers to remember about your books?
Love and art heal.

What would you do if you ever stopped writing?
Die?

Do you have any strange or funny habits?
I write. A lot.

What do you consider to be your greatest accomplishment?
Umm . . . can you guess from the answers above?

What do you wish you could do better?
Be a more patient parent.

What would your readers be most surprised to learn about you?
Not much. It's all in my books.

This companion to *Love in the Time of Global Warming* follows Pen as she searches for love among the ruins, this time using Virgil's epic *Aeneid* as her guide.

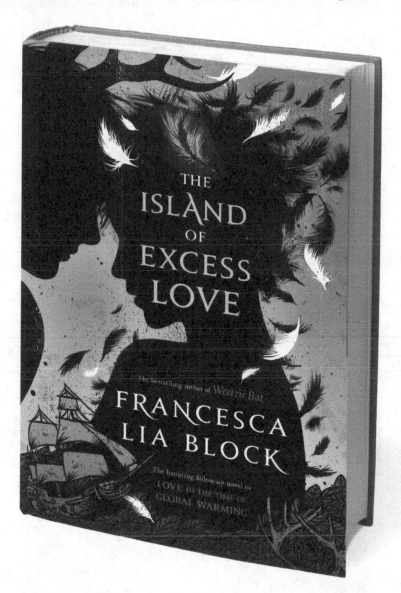

Keep reading for a sneak peek.

1

CONFLAGRATION

NOW THAT I CAN no longer believe in God or gods or goddesses, I pray each night to my dead mother, Grace, that we will survive another day and be able to stay here in the pink house on the edge of the world, that my friends and my brother and I will be safe, the plants in our garden will continue to grow, and the water in our spring will not dry up. As far as the rest of the planet after the Earth Shaker? I don't even know where to begin. . . .

My parents weren't religious, but before each meal when Venice and I were little we would hold hands and say, "Thank you for the food, god and goddess," our own tiny prayer. I guess all the myths my parents read us were a kind of religion. The myths and the images in the art books my mother collected. But there aren't many books or paintings left now. My friends and I intend to make as many of our own as possible.

Ezra—or Ez, as we call him—is our resident painter. Today he is painting another portrait of Ash who poses draped in a sheet, his feet bare and firmly planted, his dreadlocks tied back, his eyes darkly seductive. The final painting, inspired by the symbolist painter Franz von Stuck, will depict Ash as an angel winged and playing a horn; I've seen the sketches. It's appropriate to paint Ash with those broad gold wings because he told us that when the Earth Shaker hit, the wind blew him across the desert and landed him inside the body of the T-Rex statue in Cabazon where we found him. The horn in the painting will symbolize Ash's musical powers; he once charmed a monster into submission with it.

Ez has superpowers of his own; during the Earth Shaker he was able to save himself from being crushed by a toppling bookcase.

And there's the power of his art, which, in its realism and magic, seems almost as mysterious.

Ez took the wings from his imagination and memory but at least he has a real young man to paint, and one he adores at that. I'm not sure if there are any winged creatures in this world, let alone many other young men. In the days since Ez and Ash and Hex returned to me from the dead—or so it seemed—we haven't seen anyone else. I'm relieved every day that no one has come looking for us, trying to harm us or steal our food, but relief turns to a cold hollow in my belly when I think that there may not be anyone out there to come. There may be Giants like Kutter, the one who spared my life when I told him the story of how he was cloned by his maker, Kronen. Or Kutter's brother, Bull, whom I blinded with my only weapon at the time—a pair of scissors.

I'm more relieved about the fact that we haven't seen more Giants than about anything else. There's no way to explain what it feels like to be engulfed in those fleshy, greasy palms, to smell a Giant's fetid breath or feel their blood splash against your skin. No Giants here, though, just us, as if we're in some sort of protected zone they can't penetrate. Because I think they're out there somewhere. How else could this many humans and animals have vanished so quickly? The Earth Shaker didn't kill that many on its own. I believe there are Giants savaging what's left of the world.

Ash gazes into Ez's eyes as Ez paints him; they could do this all day. Not that I blame them; I stare at Hex any chance I get. I just don't paint well enough to capture him on canvas. So instead I tell myself this running story about him, everything he says and does. Like right now: he's reading a musty copy of *The Aeneid* by Virgil in my father's old armchair, the faint light of afternoon that has broken through the omnipresent clouds coming in the window. My beloved is dressed in his usual black clothes, his so-black-it-looks-blue hair slicked back from his face, showing off his widow's peak and making his eyes look even bigger than they normally do. Hex's skin is so pale and thin you can practically see through it and sometimes I wish I really could: look right at his heart. That heart, it saved my life, just by the fact of it surviving the end of the world and finding me.

"'Excess of love, to what lengths you drive our human hearts!'" Hex reads aloud, as if he knows my thoughts. *The Aeneid* is the story of how the hero Aeneas founded Rome. When Hex discovered the book on my parents' bookshelves he freaked out and made us all read it; he still shares passages with us throughout the day. "As you may recall, that's when Aeneas betrays Queen Dido's love and leaves her to go start a new civilization." Sometimes Hex likes to play schoolteacher.

"'Excess of love,'" I say. "What is that, even? How can there be an excess of love?" I want to go over and kiss his lips. They look as soft as they feel. I imagine his sharp teeth hiding under them.

"If it blinds you to the truth. If it paralyzes you and keeps you from taking action," he says, without looking up from his book. I realize I'm jealous of an ancient Roman poet who died in 19 B.C. He was a man, too, so it shouldn't bother me; Hex is definitely all about the girls. But his remark worries me.

Sometimes, especially after losing my left eye, I wonder if I'm blind to the truth but if so I don't really care, as long as my illusion includes my loved ones.

I go over and sit at Hex's feet, running my hands up the leg of his jeans to feel the warmth on my cool skin, feel the way his calf muscles bunch up. "Come help me make dinner," I say.

"Virgil is my new favorite poet," he says, not really hearing me.

I pout, making my mouth look, I hope, like Ez's muse Ash's full lips always do, even in repose. I thought Hex's favorite poet was Homer, whose *Odyssey* seemed to parallel our lives to an uncanny extent. "Didn't you reread *The Aeneid* again last week?"

"Yes, but now I'm reading it for inspiration." Hex stops and looks up at me from under the arrow of his hairline. "I'm going to write an epic poem." And then he adds, "For you," and grins, making me forget that I was ever annoyed with him. Hex has a way of doing that. Maybe one advantage of being alone on the planet, or at least the continent, is that I don't have to compete with any pretty girls for his attention. I'm his only muse, his only lover, and he's all mine.

"Pen!"

My little brother, Venice, is shouting my name as he tromps in from the garden with our dog, Argos. I hear two boy-feet in worn-out sneakers and four prancing paws on the kitchen linoleum. "The pumpkin's ready!"

If Ez, Ash, Hex, and I are busy with our stories and paintings, my brother has the most important work of all. He's in charge of the food supply and it's like his hands are charmed; he can coax fruits and vegetables from the slushy ground outside our home. If people once considered roses or diamonds the highest compliment, now we all feel that way about a cauliflower or an apple.

Venice's pumpkin is small and round, a glossy orange color. At another time—we call it Then—we would have carved a face and put a candle inside. Children dressed as demons would have come to our door asking for candy. Now we pray every day that real demons don't come and that there will be enough food to last us through the uncertainty ahead.

In the garden, the vines grow over the gazebo Hex

and Venice built and the baby pumpkins hang like small lanterns, but we didn't expect this one to ripen so fast. Of course, Venice's garden isn't like any other so it's not that surprising. When I arrived back at this house after my journey I buried the hallowed bones of Tara, the sacred girl the Giants killed. Ever since, under Venice's care, things seem to grow in our garden as if they are charmed.

If I were a plant, I'd be charmed by Ven: his dove-gray eyes and the way he coos like a dove, too, while he works, the way he tries to hide his smile by shifting his gaze and pressing his lips together.

He's shot up in the last few months and he can outrun me when we venture out to race around the periphery of the house, but he's still my little brother. He's the one I always worried about before there was any real reason to worry and the one I thought I'd lost forever when the danger exceeded anything I could ever have imagined.

Venice, Argos, and I go into the kitchen where my mother used to cook for us. Those great dinners; I took them all for granted until she was gone, swept away by the storm that followed the Earth Shaker and then by the hand of one of Kronen's Giants. The kitchen still reminds me of my mother so much—the blue and white tiles she hand painted with flowers and animals, the big wooden table where she served us breakfast, the window overlooking the garden. Missing her doesn't feel like such a terrible thing anymore. It lets me know that her memory is still within me; she's gone but she's here, too. That's one thing my journey taught me about loss. Or maybe I just have to believe this because otherwise I would have perished from grief by now.

My parents might be gone, the sea has encroached on most of the garden, and there's no functional refrigerator or stove, but I still find the kitchen one of the most comforting parts of the house.

Venice sets the pumpkin on the counter and we admire its even striations and jaunty stem. My stomach is growling already. We might have an enchanted garden but food is still scarce these days. There are no animals to hunt even if we could bear the idea of killing one. The Giants have devoured them all. Every so often we even get secret deliveries of canned and bottled goods, candles and matches, and even clothes and shoes. We never see who leaves them in the night and I've never caught the person, though I've tried. I'm pretty sure it's Merk, whom we consider our strange-angel guardian, otherwise known as my genetic father, the one who saved me from my enemy Kronen and his men three times, although not before Kronen had taken my eye.

I put my hand up to the patch I wear, reflexively,

every time I think of how Kronen bobbed his head at me, pursing his lips, gleefully stroking that little beard; the way it felt to thrust my sword through Kronen's jacket made of dried skin and into him, into a human body, when he tried to have me killed. Killing someone is the last thing I thought I'd ever do. But I never expected my life to be like this.

Here I am, unable to consider killing an animal but I actually killed a man, using just a sword. I used to be a girl who went to high school, stayed home on weekends studying the encyclopedia, art history, and mythology, whose greatest heartbreak was an unrequited crush on my best friend, Moira, and the possibility of losing our home to foreclosure when my father lost his job. Now I'm a one-eyed killer without a father or a mother or a world. My brother and my friends tell me that I'm a hero but I feel like that was all accidental and I hope it's behind me. I've learned to accept my half vision and consider the loss of my eye and my innocence the price I had to pay for being able to return to my home, find Venice, and reunite with Hex, Ez, and Ash.

They come into the kitchen as if my thought conjured them.

"Pumpkin stew?" Ez says, rubbing his hands together. He's our best chef. "I'll roast the seeds for on top and even cook the onions in some olive oil tonight." The oil appeared on the doorstep with the last mysterious delivery.

"There's kale for salad," Venice adds, pulling a dark green head of ruffled leaves from his pocket, and even Hex smiles. My junk-food lover has really changed his ways; he hardly ever mentions cheeseburgers or diet soda anymore. It's as if that life, Then, was a dream we had.

Or maybe this is the dream? As long as I have my boys with me I'll take it; I'll stay asleep.

After dinner and cleanup Hex leads us in our nightly group meditation where we sit in a circle breathing and trying to clear our minds.

Tonight Hex wants us to tell what we're afraid of and when it's my turn I say, "Having to leave here."

"Me, too," Ez echoes.

"Why?" asks Hex. He always wants to get to the root of our feelings.

"Because I don't think I can take any more of the real world," I admit.

"As long as we have each other you can." It's the first thing Venice has contributed to the discussion and makes me smile in spite of myself.

"And you're stronger than you realize, Pen," Ash adds and Ez nods and squeezes my hand.

But I don't feel strong; I feel like a small, fragile

Cyclops. Like a Cyclops, one-eyed, wrecked from battle. This Cyclops would rather go back to sleep than get up, face the world, and fight again. My expression must give that away.

"You're a storyteller," Ez reminds me. "That's heroic."

"How is that heroic?"

"Well, you make up some wicked cool words," Ash teases. "*Schnuzzle? Thrombing?* Come on, that's priceless."

"And potentially life saving," Ez contributes solemnly.

"Very funny."

Venice's gray eyes get that light-filled, dreamy look. "You have to imagine things before you can do them. Stories help us see."

"The story is the seed, the action the flower," Hex says.

"How do you define heroism?" I ask him.

"'And though his heart was sick with anxiety, he wore a confident look and kept his troubles to himself.' Virgil, speaking of the hero Aeneas who must emerge from his defeat in the Trojan War and sacrifice many things in order to found a new civilization."

"'Kept his troubles to himself.'" That pretty much describes Hex. "Which means you can't tell us what you're afraid of?"

"Bad hair?" Ash winks at Hex.

I pull on one of Ash's faunish dreadlocks. "That's you more than him."

"Well first, ow. And second, I don't want to go out there either." He frowns through the window at the encroaching night. "No matter how strong Pen here is."

"You're all forgetting your strength," Hex says, a slight snarl to his upper lip.

"You still didn't answer Pen's question," Ez challenges. "Or maybe you're not afraid of anything?"

Hex sits up straighter and glares at an invisible spot a few inches in front of his face. " 'Must you make game . . . with shapes of sheer illusion?' "

Ash flings his hair back over his shoulder. "Say what?"

"It's a passage where Aeneas is talking to his mother, the goddess Venus, who helped the Trojans. She kept rescuing her son when Athena, the goddess on the side of the Greeks, tried to harm him, but Venus always came in disguise. To answer your question, I'm afraid of illusions."

And the words crawl up my vertebrae to the nape of my neck.